An 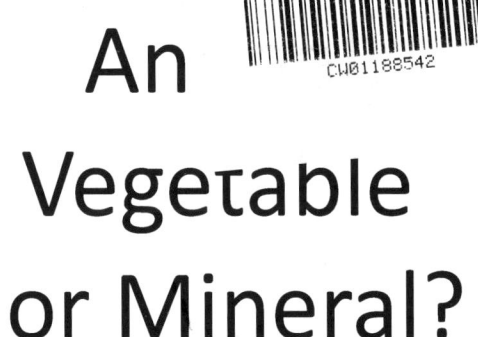 Vegetable or Mineral?

Venetia Carter

Contents © Venetia Carter 2017
Corrected edition 2018
This is a work of fiction. Names, characters, businesses, places, events and incidents are either the products of the author's imagination or used in a fictitious manner. Any resemblance to actual persons, living or dead, or actual events is purely coincidental.

www.facebook.com/WhatVenetiaWrites

ISBN-13: 978-1975679552
ISBN-10: 1975679555

Set in Palatino linotype 10.5

Cover design by George Terry
www.facebook.com/WhatGeorgeDesigns
Cover image: botanical pumpkin, public domain

Acknowledgements

Thank you to my writing partner, Josie, for helping me take the first step and for sharing the journey.
Thank you too to Kathy, Bridget, Kit, Spanna, Rachel and Allie for their helpful comments and suggestions.
And thanks to Andy for his unfailing encouragement.

Contents

Moving Back 1

House and Garden 4

Settling In 7

A New Chapter 10

Living with Mother 16

The Trouble with Boys 19

The End of a Line 23

Time for Action 29

Decluttering 32

Self-Sufficiency 37

The Compost Heap 40

Jozef 44

Winter 49

Spring 51

Coming up for light 56

Flourishing 58

A Couple of Kids 60

The Night Garden 64

Progress 70

Pumpkin soup 73

Trial and Error 81

Something Familiar 86

A Quick Dip 91

An Invitation 95

Presents 97

Jozef is Off 104

Christmas Eve 107

Christmas Day 108

Christmas Dinner Prelude 110

Christmas Dinner Itself 115

The Secret Garden 118

Boxing Day 122

Seven Magpies 125

Later that Day 128

Disclosure 131

Lengthening Days 136

News from Down Under 138

Making a list 140

Putting Down Roots 144

Arrivals 150

Two Women 155

Departures 159

A Surprise for Monica 167

Coming To 171

Seven Magpies Again 175

A New World 181

Alone at Last 184

Getting Up 187

The Sea 190

Selling Up 194

Community service 198

Moving Back

When Monica moved back to live with her mother, right back to her old room in the old family home, she found herself overwhelmed with a sense of failure. It was as though she had achieved nothing between her unremarkable childhood and the now necessary return home. She was forty three. Her daughter had married and moved half a world away. She had no house and no real career. There was no husband, villainous or heroic, or common or garden, that she could point to and say look, that one is mine. She had thought she was content but, staring at the familiar whirlpools of the Artex ceiling of her childhood bedroom, found it hard to remember why.

Still, what else was an only daughter to do? The call of duty was all but deafening as her mother had declined, falling, failing to remember, trembling with the effort and fear of the kitchen step. Her frailty cast a spell over her daughter that had more power to move her than love or guilt would have done. Of course Monica had given in.

Her mother had been a tall, heavy woman, but in her later years had contracted in all directions, folding back in on herself like damp sugar paper. The decision that Monica should return home had emerged between them as a practical solution. There was a need to have someone on hand if she fell, a need for someone who could lift the vacuum upstairs, someone who could get to the shops when the pavements were untrustworthy with ice, or the wind felt like a hand waiting to give you a spiteful shove. Rather than face the indignity of letting in a team of most likely foreign carers, Monica's mother naturally preferred the familiarity of her only child. It seemed to her that a daughter owed a mother that much. She saw nothing in her daughter's life that would be a bar to her doing her duty.

For Monica there were financial advantages in the move. She was willing to save the rent money every month. Who wouldn't be? A librarian's wages don't leave much space for manoeuvre or holidays. Assuming she could find a similarly paid job locally, she calculated her incomings and outgoings and found that her duty would be rewarded in this world. She thought this would be sufficient compensation for what she would lose.

She was nothing if not practical, so she cleared out her old bedroom. Out went the accumulation of stuff that had grown up in her absence: unwanted and unused Christmas gift gadgets, broken-backed chairs, a dusty cut glass vase of fraying silk roses, and a big M&S bag full of wire coat hangers. Then she routed out the traces of her childhood and adolescence that still lingered. She binned the once-loved cuddly orange cat toy that she found dusty and battered, brutally stuffed in a drawer mysteriously full of tablecloths. They had never used tablecloths; why were they here? From behind the bedside cabinet, she fished out a denim pencil case. It bulged with the shapes of her old felt tips, now surely dried-up. The fabric was covered with her biro stars and slogans, but with a dark ink stain blotting out one end. Holding it by finger and thumb she dropped it in the bin bag. On the chest of drawers was the mirror whose gilt frame she had painted black with nail varnish one troubled and experimental evening. That too had to go.

She redecorated the room in aubergine and soft elephant grey, replaced the faded curtains with blinds and moved in her adult possessions. Despite all this, a taint of humiliation remained, like the unevenly brown damp stain that reappeared through the new emulsion just under her bedroom window.

As she busied herself in the house, adjusting it to her

and her to it, she rested her mind on the garden. Her flat hadn't even had a balcony. In recent years she had yearned for a garden like for a wandering lover in a storybook, a lantern lit each evening so he might find his way home to her at last. The internet had provided endless varieties of horticultural pornography, and she had, through the gardenless years, indulged herself without restraint. As she had lain alone in her bed, waiting for sleep, she had woven elaborate, productive and beautiful gardens in the air from her fertile imagination: beds raised by railway sleepers, reed beds to recycle the greasy grey water from the kitchen sink, handmade homes for hedgehogs and bees, glamorous vegetables and useful flowers. The only things that had stood between her and her dreams were time, money, experience, and lack of a garden.

Although she was now to be companion, carer, cook and cleaner to her mother, by doing so, she, at last, would have a place where she could mould her solitary fantasies into vegetable life.

House and Garden

The house that was to be her home again was situated in a quiet street on the edge of a fictional town in Surrey called Mayham. It had, let's imagine, a railway station that straddled a metal trail connecting the capital with the coast. Blessed with good communications, it was likewise cursed with a population that increasingly commuted from rather than lived there. Since Monica had left in such a hurry as a teenager, Mayham had gone upmarket, warmed by the rosy glow of a prospering London. New homes had been built on the school playing fields and old ones had been extended down the gardens. Even the sold-off council houses had extruded uPVC porches and conservatories so you could hardly tell any more. In the more extensive gardens, small swimming pools and granny annexes had popped up. People didn't seem to walk much any more: shiny, fat beasts of cars transported them safely and anonymously from A to B.

The town centre too was touched by the passing years. The high street survived but with the butchers and the bank displaced by coffee chains and giftware outlets. The library, once housed in an intricate and draughty Victorian Gothic red-brick building, was now conveniently located in a glassy new shopping mall. Once a fortnight, a farmer's market gave a veneer of continental sophistication to the broad pavement opposite the new council offices.

Half an hour's walk from the town centre shops, there was a street much like the others leading to and from it. Houses had been built along it in a piecemeal fashion in ones, twos and fours over the last century. Some were packed in on narrow plots and others sat comfortably detached. Monica's mother's house was one of a pair. It was smaller than most, yet decent enough, with two good-sized bedrooms, two reception rooms and a small kitchen. It was pebble-dashed and painted white, not quite old enough to be considered pretty. Monica's parents had moved there when she was two. She knew every inch of it.

Behind a low brick garden wall, there was a small front garden bordered on the left by a gravel path that led to the front door. The rest of the space was taken up by a concrete slab relieved not one whit by a diamond-shaped hole in the middle housing a straggly yellow rose bush. The rose bloomed reliably but in a blowsy way, freely shrugging off pale petals each time a little breeze came along. Ground elder, grass and horsetails grew up wherever and whenever they had the chance in the cracks and edges of the concrete.

The back garden stretched a good length behind the house. It was unremarkable. A privet hedge marked the boundary on the right, a shiplap wooden fence the other. Next to the back door was a small crazily paved patio sporting a spider-web-on-a-stick clothes line. Beyond that lay a fuzzy-edged roughly rectangular lawn colonised by dandelions, daisies, yarrow and plantain. Around the lawn was a flower border dotted with miscellaneous shrubs. At the very end of the garden stood a wide apple tree planted by Monica's father.

Her father had been a keen gardener but, since his death, her mother had done the gardening like she did the vacuuming, regularly and in an adequate manner in order to be able to say with some truth that this job too had been done. She just wanted the garden to look nice. With irritation, she pulled out the obvious weeds that she could reach and with unwarranted optimism bought shoddy plants from the pound shop. These she planted in the bare, dry, shady patches where nothing survived or in happy nooks where they grew so well that they overwhelmed their neighbours. By the time Monica moved in, the garden had begun to relax and stretch into its own being, the strong jostling the weak, the fast taking territory from the slow, the bushes spreading themselves outwards like bacterial cultures in a Petri dish.

In contrast to the house, Monica was too old to be considered pretty. Even as a young woman though, it is not a word that would have come to mind. Her frame was too tall and broad for that, her nose too wide and her lips too thin. Sometimes her thick, dark hair looked alive as it waved down to below her shoulders, but it was too wild to be princess hair. Heavy-chested from an early age, she had as a shy teenager got into the habit of rounding her shoulders to shelter herself. By middle-age, however, she had grown a big enough sense of her own competence to look the world in the face whenever she chose to do so. This solid core and her quiet demeanour meant she appeared reliable, so, when looking for a part-time job after the move to Mayham, she had been taken on quickly by the local authority to work in the shiny new library and information centre.

Settling In

One of Monica's first jobs when she started to live again with her mother, was to deal with the smell that had built up in the house in recent years. Its origin was impossible to determine. You might describe it as an animal smell, but not like dog or horse. There was a high note of cough sweet or chest rub to it, like a sickly child in a dusty room where the windows had been painted shut. So, Monica wiped and cleared and opened windows, but the smell remained. Her mother grumbled at the draughts. Daunted but desperate, Monica launched an all-out bleach attack on washable surfaces and went to town with the laundry and the carpet shampoo. The odour diminished but lingered at the edge of perception. Reluctantly, she turned to air fresheners which helped to mask it but, whenever she came through the front door, she gave a dissatisfied sniff as she hunted it out beneath the synthetic lavender.

"What would you like for dinner, Mum?" she would enquire solicitously each day.

"Oh, I don't mind. Whatever you like, dear," came the reply. When dinner time came, though, the meal never seemed to quite suit and her mother pushed and prodded the food dubiously before eating never quite all of it, saying "Thank you, dear, that was lovely."

Despite the increasingly disfiguring entropy apparent in the garden, her mother liked to maintain her directorial role there as well as in the house after Monica moved in. In the garden, however, Monica found it harder to bear. Falling back into childhood habits, Monica resorted to subterfuge to get her way and discreetly pulled out some of the plants she particularly disliked and replaced them with her own choices. Out went the grape hyacinths with their little blue beehive flowers on hollow stalks waving insolently above their straggly, snakey nests of poor-me leaves. In their place she planted nasturtiums, their burnt orange flowers blazing covertly under the spicy foliage. After the rain, she would find herself mesmerised by their bone-dry leaves holding raindrops like miniature crystal balls reflecting in a fish-eye the world around them. From time to time she would apparently accidentally crush the odd begonia whose fleshy leaves and inelegant pink flowers irritated her. The next day, in its place would be a sunny-faced, frilly, French marigold casting its undecipherable perfume in the air as she knelt before it.

She watched each plant with keen and patient interest as the year turned so that she might discover how it fared in drought and frost, and how it suffered soundlessly as the slugs, the woodlice and the caterpillars consumed it. She discovered how profligate were the intricate seed heads of love in the mist and how the delightfully fragrant lemon balm was an invasive thug not to be tolerated outside of a pot. She diagnosed the disfiguring damage of wind burn and found with horror the perfect creamy round bodies of immature vine weevils in the crumbly brown compost of a dying potted hosta.

By the end of her first season with a garden, Monica had worked out that the pictures of somehow indecently pristine gardens on the internet and in the glossy books she had indulged in from remaindered book shops, those pictures that had fuelled her dreams and ambitions, were lies. She could see now that they bore as much resemblance to an actual garden as a high-resolution clip of a gasping, groaning perfect couple, waxed and tanned, does to a fumble and grope in the multi-storey between people who would have done better to remain as neighbours or colleagues. Despite this, she did not lose heart and came to realise that the imperfect world of slugs and multi-storey car parks was actually more engrossing than the glossy version.

A New Chapter

In the early days of moving back, Monica's thoughts would often turn to the day when she had left home. It had been a pale Tuesday at the beginning of October 1980. She was eighteen.

Her friends were arriving at their universities and polytechnics, driven there by parents in cars stuffed with belongings, but she had slipped off the train alone at Worthing station. The words of the note she had written and left behind on the kitchen table were merry-go-rounding inside her head: "sorry", "pregnant", "don't worry", "I'll be in touch". Under and in between these trite phrases was a rhythmic beat of "shit, shit, shit." As the train pulled away from her, she shook her head to chase the words away for a minute so she could consider her options. She couldn't get a taxi as she didn't know where she was going. The bus driver too would want to know the name of a road or a corner pub. So, she would walk. She shouldered her backpack and picked up her holdall and followed the last passengers towards the exit.

Worthing may seem an unlikely place for a young woman on her own with a bun in the oven. It was then, and still remains, an old-fashioned and slightly faded seaside town with a pebble beach, a Victorian pier, and well-kept floral displays. It seemed just right to Monica. She knew it from occasional family days out down to the seaside when she was a child. After a long, hot, stuffy car ride, the door would open and they would spill out to spend a sunny day on the beach, leaving, it seemed, all their troubles behind. Although Monica was carrying her trouble with her in her belly, she still thought of it as a place of escape. She hoped she could slip in unnoticed, that she could find somewhere cheap but not dirty to live.

And she felt the need for the sea, a grey and rhythmic edge making a counterpoint to all the mess of humanity that might otherwise overwhelm her.

Emerging from the station, she set off for the sea. She felt her way towards it, heading downhill and towards the emptiness of a horizon that she thought she could sense even through buildings. In time she caught patches of it, halfway up the sky between pebble-walled Victorian villas and modern blocks of flats.

The town proper lay in her path; she came across a pedestrianised precinct with wide, flat, modern shops. It had some bustle about it, enough to hide her, she hoped. She shifted direction along the shopping street and headed through and then out of town to find some cheapish out-of-the-way kind of place where she could stay the night.

A little distance from the centre, where the shops and restaurants began to be interspersed by houses, she picked a road that led again down to the sea. Along it were three or four B&Bs, all with vacancies signs in the window. She walked past them to the bottom of the road. Then she walked back up the road again and went up to the one that looked least smart. The paint on the windowsills was peeling and the white walls were dingy compared to its neighbours. The single window downstairs was fringed with flouncy net curtains, dimly revealing a dining room crowded with a few small tables. But its tiny front garden was surprisingly, at this end of the year, full of plants in pots; orange, mauve and white chrysanthemums bloomed healthily, edged with marbled ivy. And the front door gleamed smartly enough in a freshly painted black.

Boldly, as there was no other way she could do it, she rapped on the door. A little dog started yapping inside, followed by the sound of a woman's high voice telling it, "That's enough! That's enough!" Monica squeezed the handle of her holdall. She had never done this before, got herself a room. Would the woman be able to tell?

The woman turned out to be thin with dark, curly hair, bright pink lipstick and eyes made startling by make-up. She had some kind of foreign accent that Monica couldn't place. She welcomed Monica in and showed her the dining room. The dog followed them, barking neurotically from a safe distance. It was some kind of pug with a crumpled, flat face and big eyes like an ugly baby. Would her baby be ugly? Would it matter?

Now she was on this side of the net curtains she could see that the walls were lined with shelves loaded with ornaments, wide-eyed dolls in lacy dresses, pictures of kittens looking kittenish in curvy gold frames, and smooth, cool, china dogs.

"Breakfast is served between half-past seven and nine o'clock. Full English. I've only got two other guests at the moment, so there'll be plenty of room." Monica murmured, smiled, nodded. The pug gave up.

Monica was shown up narrow stairs, carpeted with dizzying turquoise and brown swirls, to a dark corridor on the first floor. Ahead of her, the landlady opened a door at the front of the house and light broke in. She followed her into the room and looked around.

The room was narrow and tall. There was a single bed with a pink and orange flowery bedspread. At its side was a dark wooden cabinet with a bedside light and a digital radio alarm clock. There was a small chest of drawers under the window on which rested a tray holding a half-size kettle, a cup and saucer, one stainless steel bowl of teabags and sachets of coffee and another full of mini pods of milk. Somehow, the sight of the hot drink facilities lifted Monica's spirits disproportionately. It breathed of an independence to come. The room was spotless and smelt of polish. It had also been cheaper than she had expected. She thanked the landlady shyly but sincerely and was left alone. She dumped her backpack and holdall on the single bed, bagsying it for herself. Then, new keys stuffed in her coat pocket, she closed the door behind her and went out to see the sea.

Relieved of her baggage, she floated out the front door and spread out her senses to take in her new surroundings. She stood for a moment to fill her lungs with the air of a new place. She could smell the sticky, wet saltiness of the sea. The weather was mild for October, lightly clouded, damp and scarcely breezy. The sea was a patch of blue-grey at the end of the road. She hurried towards it, crossing the busy seafront road to the wide promenade. There were still bright flowers in the municipal beds, but when she got up close she saw the petals were windblown and torn. She stepped past them and onto the rounded crunch and grind of the ankle-twisting shingle.

Once on the beach she could see that the sky was enormously wide and miles and miles high, a sweet baby blue hiding the dizzying blank blackness of space. Broken, whitish-grey clouds drifted along, carelessly carrying water through the air. Beneath the sky lay the sea; its glinting, shifting surface spread out massively before her. She stood and watched it, absorbed by the ragged rhythm of the waves as they noisily mounted the beach and then fell back again, dragging the pebbles with them. The odour of drying seaweed and the dizzying ozone from the violent intersection between air, stone and salt water swirled into her. The smell was vast but utterly neutral.

Her imagination dived into the water. She pierced the stretchy skin of the waves and passed into the dark silence that lay beneath. The water fitted around her perfectly, holding and pressing her. She felt the weight of billions of tons of cold water moving around her. She closed her eyes and sensed the movement of currents within currents, pulling and pushing invisibly and enormously, stretching across the Channel and beyond to the North Sea and Atlantic, as though they had no end. The eddies and flows transposed themselves onto her body as she stood on the shore, and she felt the heave and the draw of them push and pull at her organs and limbs.

Then she lost the moment. She blinked her eyes open and looked about her. The tide was high and there was no sand to speak of. She made her way down towards the dry edge of the tide line, marked by fragments of blue rope and rusty drinks cans. She sat down on the stones. There she stayed for a long time hugging her knees and focussing on losing her mind again in the deep rolling crash and high rattling suction of the waves as they reached out to and retreated from the beach. As she sat hunched and becalmed, the notion came to her that the sea was a huge amorphous beast, waves breathing as she breathed. Or a thankfully pitiless god that afforded her the choice, if she only walked towards it, of a watery annihilation and reabsorption into the simpler mineral world, a release from the biological time bomb she had become. She pictured her bloated, drowned body pulled apart by fish, becoming part of the unseen fish-eat-fish world. She chuckled inside at the notion that day-trippers might have some of her with chips on the pier one day.

Waking the next day in the strange bed, she felt cleaned out, scoured into freshness like yesterday's burnt pan. The sheets were fresh and smelt of an unfamiliar soap powder. The early morning light looked warm, filtered through thin orange curtains. Fire regulations posted on the back of the door spoke of an ordered and benign human world. She soaked up the anonymity of the room whose ugly furniture had nothing whatsoever to do with her. It was a room she could leave as easily as she had entered it.

As though it was a great treat, she got up and used the tea-making facilities provided by the establishment to make herself a cup of instant coffee and went back to bed. Propped up in her bed with a drink and the fresh light of day pushing into the room, she at last felt she could assess her situation with equanimity. She could have the baby and manage fine, she thought, as long as she could do it her way. First off, she needed a proper place to stay and money to live on. So she walked into town to sign on at the DHSS office and get herself a bedsit paid for by housing benefit.

Living with Mother

Overall, living with Mother was, as you'd expect, a sore trial. As the years of their second cohabitation crept by, the list of conditions grew longer: arthritis, hearing loss, cataracts, oedema and chronic heart failure. Each had its own demands and medication. The arthritis twisted and disfigured her hands and made walking slow and unsteady. The pain of moving took all her strength to bear, leaving her worn out. The oedema that made her ankles and calves swell until her legs were two fat parallel sausages was a symptom of her failing heart. Water tablets were prescribed which reduced the swelling but added to the number of toilet trips. As her heart failed, her breathing tried to compensate. Her cells called out for oxygen like millions of microscopic baby birds, each one a blind and unlovable gaping mouth. She gasped as though she had run a mile, in, out, in, out, after each tiny necessary excursion from her chair. Opiates helped with this but left her dreamy and confused. The mistiness from the cataracts did not yet make too much impact as she had always preferred the television to a book and could see the screen as much as she felt she needed to. She compensated for hearing loss with the television remote control. When the stairs became not just challenging but downright hazardous, Monica shifted the furniture to make the front room into a safe bedroom for her mother.

Monica's heart swelled up with pain and pride to see her mother struggle to maintain her independence in the face of the insults that time and biology threw at her. She would stand behind her as she limped around the house holding grimly on to furniture or sliding a crippled hand along the wall, over time creating a greasy strip across the woodchip wallpaper. It reminded Monica of the time spent watching her little Kate toddle around, only for her mother a fall meant shame and perhaps a fracture, instead of tears that would be soon forgotten. When alone in her bedroom, Monica would find herself half-listening out for the movements of her mother below, quick to notice any aberration from the normal routine. Curiously, all this daily care and worry fostered a tenderness, which might as well be called love, that was previously absent from Monica's feelings towards her mother.

Little by little, Monica added gadgets and handles around the house to assist her mother. She bought special cutlery with fat, curvaceous handles, a screw-on white plastic raised toilet seat, a walking frame. Each device made a positive difference, but as the technology went one step forward, her mother went two steps back.

One day, a delivery van brought a large box to their door. When it was revealed to be a commode, ordered online by Monica, her mother had bad-temperedly laughed off the necessity of such a step and made Monica put it in the garden shed out of sight of any visitors. However, one morning not long after, Monica's mother said to her meekly,

"Perhaps the commode is a good idea."

"OK Mum, I'll bring it in and we can work out a good place for it," Monica replied, as relieved as her mother.

Mother's social life gradually diminished as her and her friends' mobility stuttered and failed. The bittersweet visits of and to the women she had shared her family life with became phone calls. Names were crossed out of the ancient red leather address book. The daily tablets and ointments multiplied to crowd the dresser with squat brown bottles and white plastic tubs. Needed increasingly at home, Monica's hours at the library slipped gradually from part-time to no-time, each little loss regretted but inevitable. In this way, as her mother's life shrank, so did

Monica's.

Monica found some compensation for her diminishing independence in the garden where her influence grew commensurately. She persuaded her mother that a blackcurrant bush would look just as nice as the fruitless flowering currant. And wouldn't it be lovely to have a little herb garden by the back door? She pruned hard in winter and weeded thoroughly through the summer. A plastic compost bin appeared in the back corner of the garden. Twice a year it gave buckets and buckets of lovely mulch. The garden was not the blank canvas Monica had craved, but she was determined to transform it into something remarkable.

The Trouble with Boys

The boyfriend's name had been Diarmuid and that was a big part of the appeal. Floppy hair and an Irish accent had sealed the deal as far as Monica was concerned. He was imbued with all the glamour of having already left school.

They had met at a sixth-form party where a few drinks of cider had left Monica feeling voluptuous and a teeny bit sick. Diarmuid noticed her availability and her generous cleavage and made a move. Monica couldn't believe her luck. They snogged and he ran his hands over her to see how far he could go. She thrilled and offered only token resistance. When it was time for her to go, he gave her his phone number on a bit of card torn from the inside of a packet of ten Benson and Hedges. She kept it carefully and looked at it very often. She told no one. A long two days later, she called him from a phone box and they arranged to meet in town the next Saturday afternoon. She had just turned eighteen and was ripe for the picking.

Over the next short weeks, her tender heart, like her pale shaved legs, had opened to him fully and unconditionally and without much consideration of his past or her future. That it had been a mistake was not something she ever admitted because her soul had trembled and she had revelled in falling from her lonely world into his. Was any price too much to pay for this? She didn't think so.

Contraception had been a hit and miss affair in the first few entanglements on the warm late spring afternoons while his parents were out at work. Her A level revision had suffered, but she did enough, she hoped, to get the grades she needed for university. Already she was wondering though how she could possibly leave him.

Luckily this did not prove to be a problem.

Her missed period was a blow to her tremulous elation, but it struck her that perhaps it would bind him to her and they could forge a crazy, hippy, poor but happy future together. Unsurprisingly, that was not to be. Diarmuid had too good a head on his shoulders to commit to a big-breasted girl who had allowed herself to be pulled into bed so easily as Monica. Offering to pay for an abortion was his way of doing the decent thing. He had then dumped her simply by dint of getting his mum to say he was out when she phoned.

As summer pulled away properly, she saw him from behind at a bus stop one memorable day. He had both arms around a petite girl with short, blond hair. Monica had turned round and walked in the opposite direction, head down, mouth working hard to not cry out in pain or anger. The next day, after a sleepless, wet-pillowed night, she was in a daze, unable to escape from the reality that was banging around in her head so hard that she wanted to break it open.

This was how Monica's tender heart was ripped out and trampled. She felt sick and would have sworn it was her injured heart, not the hormones of early pregnancy that was the cause. She stopped eating, but then was assaulted by a fierce appetite so she gobbled cakes and chocolate in a fury of pain and self-destruction. She felt so humiliated that she could not bring herself to confide in anyone. In the street and in the television adverts, previously invisible babies multiplied before her eyes: crying, smiling, waving their graspy little hands with those tiny, tiny fingers. In fear of a future that was suddenly abundantly clear, she made the doctor's appointment that was too late to do her any good at all.

By the time she had moved into the bedsit on Amaryllis Terrace, West Worthing, Monica was on her way to making the best of a bad lot and finally felt secure enough to phone her mother. She waited uncomfortably for her to stop crying before letting her know her new address. She joined the library and took out books on pregnancy and childbirth and read them seriously, curled up on the sofa bed in the damp late autumn afternoons. Frightened by them into fear of what a baby would turn out like if nourished only on Jaffa Cakes and chips, she swung to the other extreme and made herself careful meals of fresh vegetables, lean chicken and brown rice. She placed her hands with satisfaction on the firm swelling of her belly.

Furthermore, with much gritting of teeth, she accepted the visits of her parents. Each visit her mother brought her a bag of food and her father pressed money into her hand. Lacking chairs, they would sit on either side of her on the sofa bed and offer advice on finance and health, and make pleas for her to come home. Monica refused politely and changed the subject. They came with baby clothes that she wouldn't have chosen herself but couldn't afford to reject, so she thanked them with muted enthusiasm. The gratitude she perhaps owed them, she felt uniquely to the welfare state that housed her and gave her the means to feed herself.

Kate was finally born on the 5th March 1981. The birth was normal, that is to say completely astonishing, deeply painful and utterly transformational. As she held her daughter in her arms, Monica knew everything would be basically fine, an intuition that never left her. Slowly, the drama and mess of birth slipped into a sleep-deprived haze of oozy breasts and sour nappies that ignited not one iota of disgust. She loved the egg-shell head that latched on to her, she loved the strange baby-flesh smell and she loved the firm, pink grip of the miniature hand. She noted with sad satisfaction the resemblance in her daughter's diminutive face to her handsome, treacherous father.

Kate grew fat and bouncy. She sat up, she crawled. She squealed with laughter at bubbles and roared with rage at being picked up out of the way of danger. She rubbed rice pudding in her hair and mashed banana onto all available surfaces. She became ill suddenly and utterly, then recovered equally thoroughly. She slept sporadically, then, at last, soundly and reliably.

The End of a Line

At what point Monica decided that both she and her mother would be better off when her mother was dead is hard to say. It was a stray thought that she brushed away, that flitted back and finally stayed. At last, eight years after she had returned to Mayham, she did something about it. It was a Monday, in the middle of a drear March.

Monica was having one of her now infrequent but deeply painful and astonishingly bloody periods. She had gotten up in the night to change her towel and had only slept patchily when she got back to bed. When her alarm went off at seven, it found her groggy and confused. It was too early. It was not quite light. She tuned into the drub of heavy rain against her window; the sky was dark with cloud behind the curtain. It was to be another rainy day. It was time to get up.

She knocked on her mother's door as usual at 7.30, cup of tea in hand, smile on face.

"Yes, come in, dear." The familiar voice sounded more wobbly than usual.

Monica went in and found her mother had already got herself out of bed. She was sitting in her bedside chair in her night clothes, her hair lank and dishevelled.

"I'll help you have a shower this morning, Mum," she said as loudly as necessary. She made space for the cup on the cluttered bedside cabinet.

"Yes, yes, do." Her mother's hand fluttered nervously on her lap.

"I'll just go and get everything ready then, Mum. Your tea's just there," Monica spoke brightly, heart sinking a bit. The shower was hazardous for her mother and embarrassing for both of them. She put the heater on in the new downstairs shower-room, nipped upstairs to fetch fresh towels and then back to her mother's room to walk her to the shower. Her mother was on her feet and pulling at the bedclothes. She turned to Monica, shame-faced.

"There's a bit of a mess. I can't quite manage. You'll have to do it." Monica went over and saw that there was a wet patch on the sheet. Bloody hell. She had tried to get her mother to use a waterproof mattress protector, but her mother had complained it was too sweaty and uncomfortable. She'd have to put one on now anyway, whether her mother wanted it or not.

"Don't worry, Mum, I can sort that out. Let's just get the shower done, eh?"

"I'm sorry. I couldn't help it. I feel like a baby. I never wanted to be like this. I should have gone when your father went. What's the point of just going on and on like this?" Her voice was high and thin.

"Come on, Mum. You'll feel better when you're all cleaned up. I'll do the bed after breakfast. Don't worry. Let's get you in that nice warm shower."

Monica helped her mum in the shower. She had never quite got used to seeing her mother naked. How strange not to have seen her mother's body when she was a young and healthy woman, but to only see it now as the old flesh hung off her frame. It wasn't fair on either of them. She wondered what her life would be like when she was old. Would Kate care for her like this? She was sure she wouldn't wish it on her own daughter, but would she be able to choose? Would she find the courage to use her bus pass one last time and take a trip to Beachy Head and hobble to the edge and beyond? What a mess for a dog walker or a child to find on the flinty beach below though! Her thoughts thus engaged, she gently shampooed her mother's hair and soaped and rinsed her soft white back.

When it was all done, Monica helped her mother get dressed and settled her in the armchair that looked out onto the garden. Today, the rain darkened the sky and made even the spring flowers look drab. It seemed like the rain would never stop and that it had been raining forever. Monica hadn't been able to do anything in the garden for days.

Usually, on bad days, her mother liked to pick subtle holes in Monica's maintenance of the garden, wishing back the days when her much-missed husband had been in charge. When she offered no such wisdom, Monica expected her mother to want to move to the other chair, the one that faced the television, but she stayed, gazing at the sodden garden, quiet and withdrawn. Monica sat at the dining table and opened up her laptop to look at nursing homes again. All the nice ones, the ones that looked like hotels, were dizzyingly expensive. Mum would have to sell the house, which she would never want to do, Monica mused. She, herself, would manage. She could go back to work and find a bedsit somewhere to rent. But what would happen when the money ran out if Mum lived another ten years? A move to some squalid place at the very time she was most in need of care?

The doctor had come yesterday. Monica had called him as her mother's breathlessness had got worse over the course of the morning, making mother and daughter panicky. The examination revealed nothing new; it was the same old story of a heart that was failing to keep pace with life. The doctor suggested having an oxygen supply at home might help and said he would set things in motion. Monica felt like weeping at the notion of more medical equipment to manage and to coax her mother into using.

At 12 o'clock they ate the lunch that Monica had made, poached yellow haddock, peas and boiled potatoes. It was one of her mother's favourite meals, but one which left the house smelling fishy for the rest of the day. As they ate,

Monica made conversation.

"I got an email from Kate last night, Mum. It sounds like it's cooling down a bit there now. I think she was getting a bit fed up with the heat."

"Kate? I haven't seen her for ages. She doesn't come to visit much. I should love to see her."

"So would I, Mum, but she's in Australia, remember? It's a long way to come! She sends her love to you."

"Oh. Well, that's nice. Kate's a lovely girl. So pretty. Such beautiful hair."

Again, this was a cue that would ordinarily set her mother off on a long reminiscence, but today a silence hung there in its place. To fill it, Monica put the television on and helped her mother to the other armchair. Then she took the plates out to the kitchen and washed up. When she returned, her mother was dozing. She jerked at the sound of Monica's entry and started watching the television again, seeming not to mind or notice the discontinuity of what was on the screen.

Monica put her hand on her mother's arm to get her attention.

"Mum, I'm just going to nip into town. I won't be long. There're a few bits we need," Monica lied.

In the hallway, she put on her waterproof jacket and ankle boots. She put her head round the door to her mother's room to say goodbye.

"I'm off now, Mum. Is there anything you need before I go?"

"I'll be fine, dear. Don't worry about me. I've got the television." She smiled firmly. Monica felt a wave of guilty relief as she pulled the front door shut behind her.

She walked briskly into town through the steady rain. Once there, she went to the pound shop to see if they had anything worth having. They didn't. But she bought a packet of chocolate digestives anyway to cheer herself up.

Next, she went to the supermarket and picked up some things they hadn't quite run out of: bread, coffee, pickle and washing soda. The rain varied in intensity but did not give up.

On the way home, she stopped at a bus shelter and got out the biscuits. She slit the wrapper with her thumbnail and took one out. She perched there on the slippery red seat staring ahead, munching her way mechanically through half of the packet, like a chain smoker. Heavy with chocolate wheatmeal, she put the packet in her bag but sat on, reluctant to go home. Her womb offered her a slow lurch of pain that she closed her eyes to accept. She felt the warm stickiness of her blood ooze out onto her towel. From nowhere, an image of her mother fallen on the floor, weakly calling out her name flashed in front of her. Startled, she pulled herself up from the seat. No, there was no reason to panic, but Mum would be wanting the toilet again soon so she must head back. She wondered how much those alarm gadgets that hung around your neck cost.

In through the front door, Monica noted the tired fishy smell, but something else was mingled with it. Burning? She went to her mother's room. There she was, dozing in the chair facing the TV which was loudly explaining about improving rents for properties in the north east. The singed smell was stronger in here. There was a copy of Woman's Weekly on top of the convector heater by her mother's chair. The cover pages were lifting slightly as the warm air passed by them. The shiny paper was crinkling and when she grabbed it off, the pages were brittle under her hand. The sudden movement roused her mother.

"Oh! Oh dear! You did give me a fright!" and then, "Where have you been? I called and called but you didn't come."

"Oh, Mum. I went into town to get some bread. I told

you I was going. You can always call me on my mobile. The number's there." She pointed to the hand-printed note with "Monica's Number" written and underlined by the phone on the little table next to her mother's chair.

"I didn't think of it. I do wish you wouldn't go away for so long."

"I know, Mum, but I have to go out sometimes."

"I know that. Of course you have to. I am glad you're back. I'm sorry I'm such a nuisance. I never meant to be." All this was true.

"I know, Mum. I'm here now. Shall we see if there's a film to watch?"

"Yes, dear. I'd like that. You have on what you want. I don't mind what I watch."

Monica picked up the remote and started clicking through the channels for something her mother would enjoy.

"Mum, you really mustn't put anything on that heater. It could cause a fire, you know."

"I don't know why you're always going on about that. I never put anything on there."

Monica's frustration and anger surged up, but she beat it down, saying: "OK, Mum, but please be careful."

Monica sat with her mother while the film was on to reassure her after her earlier absence. The rest of the day unrolled in a routine way, only it seemed much longer than usual. By the evening, she felt she could not manage another one like it. Part of what was unbearable was witnessing her mother, not only suffering but sad and confused. Surely this wasn't right.

Time for Action

As a woman who valued her integrity, Monica could find no good reason not to act on her conviction that her mother's death would cut short the indignity and suffering that her ailments were subjecting her to. That the death would also relieve Monica of a burden that she was tired of carrying, made it feel like a win-win situation. The doctor had implied she could go at any time or last for years. Surely they wouldn't inspect the death of such a frail and ill person too carefully? With a pulse of action that filled her with a giddy sense of liveliness, she swapped the motley coloured contents of her mother's nightly medicine pot for a single batch of the opiates she took for breathlessness. How many was enough to kill her? Monica thought about googling it but somehow that felt too cold-blooded, like a proper murder. In the end, she put in eight, the number of pills she normally took at that time. It felt like she was giving her mother a fighting chance to survive, like giving her a gentle push that might or might not make her fall down a flight of stairs. Her mother didn't seem to notice the exchange of medication, but of course, she may have colluded for her own reasons. She took the white, round pills one by one by one and there, with a goodnight peck on the downy cheek, it was done.

Monica went straight to bed afterwards but did not go to sleep. Instead, she lay there rigid under the duvet straining to hear sounds from her mother's bedroom below. She listened for sounds of distress. She feared vomiting and confusion. And accusation: she did not think that she could lie about what she had chosen to do. Now she was unsure whether what she had done was right in any sense of the word. Should she go down and rouse her mother? Call an ambulance? She feared the noise and the embarrassment of reversing the murder she had set in motion more than letting it run its dastardly course. A hot, red wave of shame rose over her and she threw off the covers. She wondered at herself. She viewed her actions through the distorting lens of tabloid headlines: "Woman, 51, murders mother", "Evil Mum killer". It was some kind of mad recklessness that had invaded her; she must go down and save her, she said to herself as she lay straight and hard as a plank on the pink brushed cotton sheets. But the part of her that had no voice said nothing and did nothing.

As the night staggered on, she heard her mother's breathing become loud and ragged. A terrible pulling in and pushing out of air as though it was as thick as treacle. Like the sea, it had a hypnotic rhythm, but the meatiness of straining muscle made it horrible. It filled Monica's head, but she felt she had no right to stuff the pillow over her ears and keep it out. So she let it in and breathed with her. There was no voice of protest or of pain. If there had been, perhaps Monica would have leapt up from her bed and rushed downstairs to soothe her mother with soft words, or induce vomiting, or even to call an ambulance. But the breath was not a human voice, it was a sound made by the turbulent passing of air across a slackly vibrating tube of tissue.

The spaces between the old breaths and the new breaths grew longer and longer so that there was more not breathing than breathing, more death than life. Now, each long gap between the noisy breaths felt like it must be the last. Monica wished and wished that it would be. Still another breath came, pulling in the oxygen demanded by the starving, ancient cells, holding it in silence, and then the weary slump, pushing out the gassy waste. It was mesmerising. It was horrific. Then there was no more.

Monica realised she had stopped breathing too and opened her mouth to let out a lungful of air. She felt half-drowned, washed up on her bed in the awful silence and the dark. She curled up like a child, pulling the cover over her head, and wept with rage and fear until the night faded to grey. In the almost light, she slept at last.

When she awoke, the daylight was full and bright behind the edge of the curtains. It was late, much later than it should be. She sparked into self-awareness and memory of the night before. Had she done it or dreamt it? Neither seemed plausible. She scrambled out of bed and into her dressing gown and slippers and hurried down the stairs. She paused at her mother's door, tasting the silence for clues. She rapped on it, more loudly than she had intended. No answer. "Mum?" Nothing. Heart banging, she opened the door an inch and peered in. The familiar room was dim behind the closed curtains, but she could make out from the strange slack expression on the face on the pillow that the figure lying in the bed was no longer her mother.

Decluttering

"You were so good to her, dear. Not many daughters would have done what you did. She was lucky to have you. And she knew it." One of the few surviving friends of her mother was settled in her mother's high armchair, both hands resting on the knob of her stick. The fingers were twisted to the side at the swollen knuckles, just like her mother's had. A gold band shone smoothly on her left hand amidst the wrinkles and liver-spots. She smiled up at Monica standing before her, holding a teapot.

"Oh, I don't know about that. I just did what I could. Would you like some more tea? There's plenty in the pot." This was the last guest now. There had only been a handful who had come back to the house after the cremation. The others had made their excuses and headed off a little while ago.

"No, thank you; I've still got some here." She reached out for Monica's hand and gave it a squeeze. "She was a good friend to me, your mother; I shall miss her."

Monica couldn't find a thing to say. Her visitor took another swallow of her tea.

"Well, I'd best be off. My nephew is waiting in the car. Thank you so much for inviting me. That fruit cake was delicious!" She pushed down on the stick to lever herself up onto her feet. They bulged out of her soft fabric shoes in a heartbreakingly ugly way. Monica bent forward to rest her cheek on the cool dry flesh of her visitor. She smelt of old lady talcum powder, gardenia or rose or something.

"Thank you for coming. Let me see you to the door." Monica felt her throat tighten and her mouth wobble as she opened her mouth to speak.

A week or so later, her mother's ashes arrived from the

funeral directors in a burgundy plastic tub the size of an old-fashioned sweet shop jar. Her mother had never said what she wanted doing with them. They sat in a corner of the kitchen for the next day, catching Monica's eye as she moved around, making tea, washing up. The following morning she scooped up the tub and stepped out into the garden. She felt the sun shining down and the humidity rising up. May was broadening spring out into summer. She surveyed all the thrusting fecundity of the vegetable kingdom around her; the world was remaking itself again. She would give up what was left of her mother to the dance of life. With a heartfelt attempt at reverence, she walked up the path to the compost bin and tipped the ashes on. A lick of wind danced a few grey specks into her face and onto her clothes and dusted the nearby grass. She wiped them off herself as though they would hurt her if they stayed. Unsettled, she snatched up her garden fork and stuck it into the pile, mixing in the ashes so the potash and phosphate would be well-distributed and any toxins would be diluted by vegetable peelings and weeds.

Monica's next few weeks were taken up in the financial and legal dealings and house-clearing that such times entail. Her mother's absence from the house was a relief, though she felt loss too. She toyed with grief and guilt but felt that neither of them quite fitted her. More than anything else she felt unshackled and required that the place she inhabited reflected this. Starting with her mother's bedroom, she cleared.

She sold off and gave away the furniture. Smaller items like books and ornaments she examined critically, and then, with few exceptions, she consigned them to someone else's future rather than her own. Some things were so stained or broken that she left them outside in the hope that someone would take them and someone generally did. With a heave and a dust mask, she pulled up stained and worn rugs and carpets. Their faded patterns were imprinted onto her mind's eye so that even when they were gone, their ghosts remained a second glance away from the present. The bare floors she revealed were dusty and spiked with wicked twisted black tacks and pocked with old tack holes. Traces of floor coverings past were printed on the boards: the mesh of old linoleum, worn paint on the edges of stair treads, and the sticky, dark adhesive from tiles. Many of these predated her family's occupation and provided her with a comforting historical perspective on her mother's passing and that of her own to come. The house stood in bricks and mortar disdain as lives flitted through it like flimsy daddy longlegs. She got off what she could, banged in the tack heads and left it at that.

Her mother's clothes she found peculiarly distasteful to handle. Did tiny fragments of her mother's skin cling weakly to their fibres? She bundled them into bin bags and, under cover of darkness, left them one at a time outside the Salvation Army shop. She had a feeling she ought to have washed them first but baulked at the chore. She acknowledged the bad karma she was thereby accumulating and promised the universe to make it up in some way. The house plants that had survived her willful neglect she threw in the compost bin. They felt like battery hens caged so long that they were beyond rehabilitation.

She opened all the windows and left them open, even in the rain. The air pushed in from outside and then passed out again, carrying old smells and dust. In came damp air from late spring showers, the scent of wallflowers, pollen from the neighbourhood daffodils, fine particles from car exhausts and the sounds of children playing out in the warming weather.

Once she had cleared, she cleaned. Rubber-gloved, she wiped down the walls, standing on a stool to reach the greasy cobwebs near the ceiling. Up and down, bucket and rag, sugar soap and hot water, until she was tired out.

When each room was empty and clean, she painted the walls white and moved on to the next. In time, she looked around her own bedroom and decided she would do the same there. She folded and cajoled the mattress downstairs to the now bare front room where her mother had ended her days. She slept uneasily there while she whitewashed part of her own past into history. The next day, with the smell of the paint still thick in the air, she dragged the mattress upstairs again.

For the last couple of weeks, she had been wearing work clothes all day – tops with old stains on and trousers that were past mending. When she looked at her clothes in her wardrobe and chest of drawers they seemed to belong to someone who wasn't there anymore, much as her mother's had. So, in turn, she bundled most of her old clothes, some cherished and some ghastly mistakes, into the black bags for the charity shop too. She thought she would like some kind of uniform like in Mao's China or secondary school which meant she wouldn't have to bother with all that decision-making in the mornings about what kind of person she was that day. She looked around for clothes that would excite no particular curiosity or admiration and would give her the anonymity of a hijab without the abuse that would go with it. In daylight this time, she went to the charity shop where she was both relieved and ashamed not to find any of her mother's clothes (had they put them all in the wheelie bin or had they been snapped up by vintage-seeking shoppers?). She bought several pairs of jeans that more or less fitted, some fleeces (navy, bottle green and grey), loose cotton shirts for hot weather and a nearly-new waterproof jacket for the rain. What do your clothes say about you, Monica? They say: I couldn't give a fuck.

She left sorting through the photos until last. Eventually, everything else had been done and she pulled out the drawer filled with shoeboxes, envelopes and albums and took it down to the kitchen. She spread the images out on the kitchen table, making piles of keepers and throwers. The keeping pile was too big. From them, she chose twenty, which she put in an envelope in the bottom drawer of her chest of drawers. The rest went in the bin. In the middle of the night, she got up and put the ones in the envelope in the bin too.

In the morning, she fished them out and posted them to Kate in Australia. Kate had offered to come back for Granny's funeral, but Monica had persuaded her that the expense was unnecessary. Monica couldn't see the point in her travelling all that way for such a sad event. What's more, she now felt she had a secret from Kate and was not ready to share it.

Self-Sufficiency

Now that the house was sorted, Monica could finally allow herself to focus on the garden. Starting at the far end of the garden, she raised a series of beds for the plants she hankered to grow: rhubarb, squash, garlic, potatoes and alpine strawberries. The lawn shrank until it was nothing more than a set of grassy paths between metre-wide beds, shored up with scaffolding planks. As the spring advanced, she sowed and transplanted to fill the beds. She moved the compost heap from the bottom of the garden to the centre to reduce unnecessary footsteps.

She would wake early in the mornings, guided by the sun rather than the clock. Sometimes she would doze a little, especially on rainy days, but otherwise would get herself up and dressed for the day. She made herself porridge sweetened with a big spoonful of homemade jam from the unlabelled stack in her larder. Morning was the time for tending and remaking the garden.

Under her close supervision, the plants flourished and the snails and caterpillars were crushed swiftly under sensible shoes, smearing their mysterious organs across the path.

When she had done all that needed doing in the garden and a little beyond that, she had her lunch. Lunch was often soup made with whatever there was from the garden. After lunch, she found that she enjoyed putting her feet up and drifting off a little while listening to Radio 4 or the subdued neighbourhood sounds that seeped in through the window. Later in the afternoons, she made the most of her dwindling money by managing her resources. Twice a week, she would walk the two miles to the supermarket and hunt for bargains and top up on her basic foodstuffs. Afterwards, she would trundle her shopping trolley the two miles home. Other days, she would bake, mend things that had broken, clean and tidy the kitchen and do her laundry by hand. She made a moderate effort for her evening meal: laying the table nicely, making pretty salads, putting a sprig of fresh mint in her glass of water. After dinner, if it was still light and fine, she would return to the garden and tinker or sit on the lone white plastic, pointlessly stackable chair and inhale the pollen grains and the volatile molecules released by her increasingly luxuriant garden. You could say that her existence was self-centred, but that was just because she had taken some care to position herself there.

By the end of July, Monica had exhausted her savings and the cash her mother had left in her purse and in envelopes around the living room, and started a small overdraft. She had eaten most of the food that was in the cupboard and freezer, enjoying the oddness of the meals she prepared as the stock reduced – baked beans and rice with pickled onions; porridge and tinned peaches; soup made from gravy granules and tinned tuna. At last the freezer was empty, so she sold it and used the money to buy margarine, toilet roll and toothpaste. As far as she could, she used garden produce to supplement her supplies. Apples from the old tree at the bottom of the garden were a daily part of her diet. They started as hard, green, tannin-filled shockers with white pips which she stewed and sweetened with white sugar. Next came their rosy peak of sweet, pink-tinged flesh, each one gifted to her hand with the slightest twist. Finally, they were reduced to the shrunken skins and wasp-holed windfalls that marked the end of the summer bounty in a second spate of stewed apple.

The vegetables which she had covertly implanted amongst her mother's flower borders without, she prided herself, a loss of decorative value, came into their own.

Rainbow chard and fennel; tiny, tumbling tomatoes; beetroot, ferny carrots and curly kale all repaid her for the care she had taken with them since they were tiny dried capsules of vegetable DNA. She harvested them with a keen appreciation of their vegetable loveliness and cooked them sensitively, savouring the texture of their ripe flesh as it gave way to her kitchen knife. The beetroot were particularly fine: thin-skinned globes which stained her chopping board and fingers magenta and, when stewed and puréed, became a dense, earthy velvety soup. Blithely in the summer sunshine, she snipped at the marigold and nasturtium flowers to add their orangey joy to her intriguing salad plate of fennel leaves and sweet apples and young shoots of chard.

Despite her best efforts in the garden and the kitchen, the deficit in her cash supply was beginning to be a worry. Garden produce was all well and good, but the utility companies reminded her that she was tied to a cash requirement that was harder to replace. Still, she was inclined to do what she could and took fewer baths and left the plug in so she could scoop out the grey water with a bucket to flush the loo. Although the weather was cooling, she did not turn on the heating and simply went to bed when she felt chilly in the evening.

The Compost Heap

At the geometric and functional centre of Monica's garden was the new compost heap. It was a heaving, steaming engine, turbulent and mysterious. Its sides were made of pallets she had nailed together, shored up with bits of cardboard to stop things falling through the gaps and to hold the heat in its rotting belly. All the usual garden waste was deposited there. First and foremost, the weeds: the sturdy clumps of creeping buttercup roots, the fine soft stems of mouse-eared chickweed, the long-rooted dandelions prised reluctantly from their tunnels in amongst the rhubarb; and those pretty grey-green ferny ones that popped up namelessly amidst the spring sowings. Next came the near misses, the thinnings of carrots and beetroot that found themselves in the wrong place at the wrong time, the rocketing radishes and spinach that made an unbidden bid for independent procreation, and the spiny prunings of gooseberry bushes, sacrificed to give better branches the space to thrive. In summer, long grass strimmed from the paths was dumped in fragrant temporary bulk. In autumn, the heady brown windfalls spotted with cream formed a fragrant layer followed by their retinue of tipsy wasps. Next went on the brittle stalks and papery leaves from exhausted pea and bean plants, and the redundant, pale and hollow trailing stems of squash and pumpkins.

The kitchen made its own contribution to this remarkable crucible. A lidded bucket received the usual vegetable peelings. It also got teabags (ripped open to speed their decomposition), torn toilet roll inners and egg boxes, egg shells, short bits of string, perished rubber bands, the dull husks of dead flies in the spider webs that had trapped them, and the floor sweepings of skin flakes, crumbs and dirt. Out of the living room came soft, grey wood ash from winter evenings by the fire musing, reading and googling. The front door mat provided a weekly carbon supplement in the form of the free local newspaper, read for the light it shed on how other people lived their lives and then torn to digestible ribbons.

The dusty substance of Monica's mother was an unusual addition but was not alone in that. Fingernail clippings, hair trimmings and tissues used for mopping her nose were all added in. Corrugated cardboard was ripped into a bucket and left next to the toilet for a nitrogenous golden shower before being processed by the strange alchemy of the heap into miraculous dirt.

One morning, Monica found a mouse floating right way up in her water butt. It posed in a swimming stance stiffened by exhaustion and then death. She hunted round and found an old bit of wood to fish it out with. Taking care not to damage it, she lay it down on the grass and looked for some minute sign of life. Her mind's eye filled with visions of its desperate swim round and round the dark water, scrabbling at the wall of black plastic when it neared the edge but unable to haul itself out. How long could a mouse keep on? When it failed to recover, Monica made a hole in the compost heap and patted the mouse in. The mouse was gobbled up in no time, even the sardine-soft bones were gnawed away until nothing that could be seen as mouse remained.

Whenever the pile crept to the top of the palettes, Monica covered it and solicitously tucked it in with a thick sheet of black plastic. On top of this went an old rug to insulate it. Then the worms and bacteria and fungi were left to do their work of breaking complex things down into simpler ones, releasing into the core of the heap the warmth of the sun that had grown them. At its side, she built a new container, so the work could start again. By the time the second one was full, the first was ready.

She would allow herself a whole day for the pleasure of harvesting the new batch of compost. Early in the morning she lifted off the covers and sniffed the sweet, complex smell of the unmade stuff of life. Gristly slugs, basking in the moisture and warmth of the underside of the plastic, she cut resolutely in two and scraped into the younger heap. Then the sorting began. Steadily forking the brown stuff into the wheelbarrow, she threw unrotted sticks, avocado stones and as many pink wriggly worms as she could into the new heap for a second journey through the vale of unmaking. The muck that passed muster she distributed as a thick mulch around her hungry plants, one handful at a time, kneeling before them. Through Monica's agency, atomic fractions of her mother were now laid bare in the soil to be knitted by vegetable love into courgettes, rhubarb and French beans ready for the table.

The year turned its spiral into the future like a blunt corkscrew into an achingly infinite cork. Children, tanned and tall, returned to school in September. Garden swimming pools were emptied of water and tautly covered up so the curled brown leaves drifting from the trees wouldn't gather in them. Any fine and sunny day felt like a gift.

Monica's garden generously gave up its autumn produce: sturdy leeks, curly kale and bulging swedes. The nitrates, magnesium and potassium, liberated from their old lives by the many and various microscopic and macroscopic denizens of the heap, had been transformed into proteins, chlorophyll and tiny molecular pumps in the membrane of vegetable cells.

The tiger worms worked on, day and night, channelling the detritus through their annular bodies for it to emerge moistly reduced from their tiny worm anuses. Monica weeded, harvested, stored and mended. The compost heap steamed like a slow cooking pot as the year cooled and darkened around it.

Jozef

October proved to be a good month for Monica. The probate for her mother's affairs was granted so she could finally tap into the savings that her mother and father had so prudently and painstakingly built up out of the hard work and habitual economies of their married life.

With the flash of cash, Monica paid the overdue bills and restocked the toilet roll and other items on the small list of goods that she considered essential. However, it was in her nature to be frugal, and the mechanics of being such had long been a pleasure she would not now willingly forego. She counted up her money and calculated that by living in the most parsimonious fashion, she could get by without getting a job for the time being. One day her funds would run out, but she might well be dead, or at least past caring, by then. Such imprudence at her age smacked of sin, and she savoured the wickedness of it. She had tied up her life at the threshold of her adulthood with an unplanned pregnancy and then done the right thing by her mother. Now here she was unpicking the knot that was her old life patiently, quietly and relentlessly.

October brought a second change to Monica's quiet life, this one more unexpected than the first. It happened on a Wednesday.

After breakfast, Monica opened the front door to taste the weather; the grass was bowed over with raindrops, but the sun was coming out. It was a good day to go to the shops. Monica had put off the walk into town for her food shop because of the poor weather these last few days, but today would do nicely.

In the supermarket she bought rolled oats, washing-up liquid, sugar, oil, tins of tomatoes from the bright yellow economy range, some cheap speckled bananas and a short shelf-life quiche for a treat. Trolley loaded, squishy bananas on top, she exited the store.

Sitting cross-legged on the ground next to the sliding door, was a youngish man. He was leaning against the wall bathed in sunshine, a neatly rolled sleeping bag on one side and a backpack on the other. In front of him was a sign written on corrugated cardboard in a foreign language: Hungarian? Czech? She stopped to consider it. The man looked up at her, unsmiling but direct. He had blondish stubble on his head and face. He looked subtly foreign. Holding her gaze, he gestured to a red cotton kerchief knotted in each corner on the ground in front of him. A handful of coins lay on it. It was rare to see begging on the streets in this comfortable backwater.

"What does the sign say?" she asked, enunciating self-consciously and pointing to the sign.

"It says, madam, `We are all in this together`," he replied, unsmiling. He did have a foreign accent. Something Eastern European? But his English sounded good enough for him to have written the sign in English if he had wanted to.

Monica nodded in acknowledgement and, uncertain what else to do, walked on. She got to the end of the road where there was a coffee shop with sanded floorboards, fat leather sofas and art prints. Uncharacteristically, she went in and ordered herself a fancy frothy coffee. She sat by the window and looked out at the faces of the shoppers. She saw pretty schoolgirls mirroring each other's style and gestures, overweight people with their painful rolling gait as hip bone ground against thigh bone, stressed parents snapping at exuberant toddlers, and old women concentrating on the next painful step. She would fix upon one of the passers-by and briefly imagine their homes and their families, their joys and their worries. Her life seemed uncomplicated in comparison. Coffee finished, she walked back down the road to where the man sat with his sign.

"Excuse me," she said, "I think you're right," as though no time had passed since he had spoken to her. "What do you need?"

"What do I need? Not much. Money? I would like to have somewhere to sleep tonight." He squinted up at her trying to make her out, hand covering his eyes against the low sunlight shining around her.

"There's a room you can use at my house tonight. There's not a bed, so you'd have to sleep on the floor."

As they walked back to her house, Monica gently extracted his story from him. His name was Jozef and he was a chef. He had made his way from his native Slovakia to England to earn a better living than he could at home. He'd found work easily at first through a friend already settled here. The work was washing up, but he didn't mind too much; the pay was better than what he would have got at home working as the head chef and he was practising his English for free. A slip on black ice in the winter had left him with a broken arm and, despite sympathy from the restaurant owner, no job. He'd lived on his savings while his arm healed, but by the time he was fit for work, he had no money left. Failing to get another position, he got behind with the rent and lost his small room. In this way, he found himself, much to his own surprise, on the streets. All he wanted now was enough money to return home.

"It's just here," announced Monica, as the house came into view. She stepped ahead of him through the gate and up to the front door. She fished out her keys and unlocked it, then turned to smile at him. "Come in." He stepped across the threshold hesitantly.

"I'll show you where you can sleep. It's up here." He followed her up the stairs. "This was my parents' room. It hasn't been used in a while." As she looked around it with Jozef at her shoulder, it looked stark and unwelcoming like a monk's cell, white walls, bare boards, no curtains, no bed, just a chest of drawers and a large dark wooden wardrobe that had been too big to move.

"I can get you a pillow and a duvet. I'll see if I've got something to make it more comfortable."

"It's fine. Thank you. I have a mat and a sleeping bag. Thank you. You are very kind." Monica gave half a shrug. "I'll get you a towel so you can have a bath if you want to."

Jozef stayed the night. Then he stayed the next. After that, he just stayed.

As the weeks went on, he acquired things for the room. Firstly, a discarded mattress in reasonable condition left on a dry day leaning against a recycling bin. Next, a broken red anglepoise lamp which he contrived to mend. Then books, for which he built a shelf from bricks and a couple of planks. Monica shifted a little to absorb his presence in the house. It was a bit like having a lodger again, like she had done when Kate had gone to university, but without the slightly uncomfortable task of having to ask for rent. What's more, she found that having a new person stay in Mum and Dad's old room upstairs, meant it was no longer their room, but Jozef's. In this way, she achieved, without planning to, another degree of separation from her old life.

Monica's intervention provided the yin to the yang of the black ice that had been Jozef's downfall. It was a similarly unforeseen event but it meant that he bounced up rather than down. As much as he valued the practical support her act had given him, it was the essential altruism of it that really made him recover his footing in the world. At first, he had suspected her motives. Did she want a toy boy? Cheap labour? His kidneys? However, as time passed, he saw that she expected nothing from him beyond what any host would require of a guest: good manners and a falling in with the household rules. He found these a little odd, but perhaps in this curious country it was normal to gather and compost the hair from the plughole in the bath and to flush the toilet with a bucket of bathwater?

Jozef offered to help around the house and took over the washing up and kitchen cleaning. He would have been happy to cook, but Monica demurred, apparently unwilling to let him handle the produce from the garden until she had by her own capable hands transmuted it into meals on plates.

His trust in his luck restored by Monica, he went out again to look for work and in time found a job as a kitchen porter in a gastro pub. His first wages he gave entirely to Monica, who took them happily in the spirit in which they were offered. Thereafter, he left her money every Friday on the kitchen table.

Winter

Winter is the dark necessity that trims back life ready for its springtime renewal. The mineral aspect of the universe is in the ascendant again as when the world first began. The wind is untempered and howls through the streets, unmaking what it can. The rain washes away mineral ions from the soil to streams and rivers and underground canyons and onward to the sea. The sea swells and thrashes the shore, biting into the Sussex cliffs made of the chalky remains of billions of tiny skeletons. People stay at home or hurry along from shelter to shelter. Plants recede and stockpile their solar-powered starch or else die. Particles lose energy to the dark coldness of space and slow down their frantic oscillating and scudding about to a slower dance. Colliding rarely and weakly, chemical reactions, metabolic and otherwise, just don't happen like they used to in the long days of summer. Dissipation and entropy abound.

As the natural world unravels, humans use the long dark evenings to plan for better times. First of all, planning for Christmas, a lively feast in open defiance of its season, a feast that colours living rooms red and green and shiny and fills the streets with blinking lights. Christmas plans are made to visit the family, to buy stuff to stuff the stockings with and stuff to wrap it up in, and to buy food to stuff ourselves with. Plans to make it somehow magical this year for the kids and peaceful for the grown-ups.

Then more plans. Plans for sheds, plans for extensions, plans for slimming, plans for holidays in the sun, plans to not smoke, not drink, be kinder, learn the flute. Jozef is planning to get a cook at work into bed and Monica, of course, is planning her garden.

Throughout the winter, the compost heap churns away. Slower now, but nevertheless progressing in its deconstruction of things into matter. Its various populations labour away doggedly. The blind tiger worms tunnel and stir. The woodlice scuttle at the margins, gnawing grey sticks with their armoured mouths. The centipedes, like miniature Chinese dragons, hunt their gentle wormy prey. The moulds ooze their digestive juices and slurp up the resultant soup, and the bacteria, like any cells, eat, grow, divide, eat, grow, divide. The heap is a community of living things bundled in with their food and their excrement, their young and their dead, like any community. It's the great mystery through which that which was dead becomes that which will be alive again, the secret of eternal life. This great leveller unknits human and plant cells into raw material for new cells: nitrates and phosphates, magnesium and potassium, iron and calcium, water. The carbon dioxide, again unbound, drifts back out into the atmosphere. The sunlight that bound together plant and animal body parts is now returned to the cold universe. Nevertheless, as it is released, it flows warmly through the heap so that steam drifts up on the frosty mornings when Monica uncovers it to stir the edges into the centre. On one of these mornings, a child in the garden next door sees the steam rising from next door's garden and thinks about witches and cauldrons.

Spring

Spring crept in. Promised by a fine day, and broken by a gale. Yet in it came. This year, Monica felt properly ready for it. She had planned to extend the season so there was to be more produce to eat early in the spring and more to eat late in the autumn, and less to be bought from the shops. She was going to build a greenhouse.

Over the winter she had collected building materials from neighbourhood skips: timber, old windows, clear plastic sheeting and guttering. It lay disgracefully in a pile in her front garden. The front garden had thus far been neglected by Monica. Still the concrete, still the straggly rose, but now weedier than ever in the cracks and at the edges. Horsetail, hairy bittercress and shepherds purse had joined the old faithfuls of dandelion and plantain which themselves had grown taller and fatter without the insult of their usual routine injuries.

The front garden, and in particular the yellow rose bush, reminded Monica of her mother. Each time she walked past it, some memory of her mother presented itself, a kind word or an angry look or the rasping sound of her breathing through her long last night.

One mild morning at the end of February, she went out to the front and took a good look around. With the rose, she resolved that the pain that it inflicted on her might well be salutary and elected to embrace and water it rather than grub it out. She gave it a good prune and mulched it mindfully with the woody remnants of the summer heap that contained her mother's ashes. Next she set to weeding the gaps in the concrete with the old broken knife, just like she had done when her mother was alive. She gave it a proper go, digging the knife in deep and grazing her knuckles repeatedly on the concrete edges.

This done, she felt she had gone some way towards making peace with her mother's ghost.

In the afternoon, she put pots of cuttings of herbs against the wall of the house. She chose the ones that would like the hoped-for sunshine and warmth of that spot: fragrant thyme, rosemary and hyssop.

She built the greenhouse bit by bit on the days in early spring that were dry and not too windy. As she needed different materials, she carried them round to the back of the house. Up it grew, leaning against the house and sheltering and darkening the back room window.

By the middle of March, the greenhouse was finished. It had been a long and awkward job and it was clearly not a thing of beauty. Nevertheless, Monica had high hopes that it would do. The sides were made of old window frames screwed together and the roof from a sheet of corrugated clear plastic that someone had replaced with something better. She made deep eaves with the plastic sheet to keep the rain from further rotting the frames and left the gaps made by the undulations of the sheet to allow some ventilation. She had hoarded and picked up large containers to use as plant pots: big plastic oil bottles, empty white emulsion tins, tough plastic bags. These were for the crops that would live out their lives in the shelter of the greenhouse: aubergines, basil, peppers and so on, plants that came from sunnier lands. With a kitchen skewer she pierced the containers for drainage and arranged them in the new greenhouse on either side of a narrow central pathway. She lined them with stones foraged from the garden and then filled them with garden soil combined with sand and moist sieved compost from her own heap. The resultant mixture was moist, brown and even. It looked good enough to eat.

In pierced margarine tubs and yoghurt pots, filled with the same growing mixture as the big tubs, she began to sow the seeds of tender plants that she could fool into thinking that spring had come early: lollo rosso, sweet peppers, climbing cucumbers, yellow tomatoes, cape gooseberries, aubergines.

Jozef came through the winter looking healthier, happier and meatier (he'd been doing extra shifts in the kitchen, working out at the chopping board and lifting the pans). One evening as they shared a bowl of leek and potato soup (last of the leeks, potatoes from a shop) he asked shyly if she minded if he brought a friend home. It made her feel like his mother. She had no objection and found herself pleased for him and curious about who it would be.

"No, I don't mind at all."

The next night when he came in after the late shift at the restaurant she couldn't help but hear two sets of feet climb the stairs. Smiling to herself, she turned over in her bed and drew the covers up in an effort to build them a little wall of privacy. She thought wistfully of her own handful of lovers that night. There was Diarmuid, Kate's father, too handsome and too charming to stay around for long with an awkward, big-breasted girl who had got pregnant. She didn't blame him.

In later years she had felt lonely when Kate had gone to university. Restless too. Two of the foreign students that had taken Kate's room had briefly been taken to bed by her. She had made them nutritious evening meals and put a bottle of red wine to breathe on the table. Alone in this cold and windy country, they had been relieved to find such comfortable lodgings at a cheap rate and they unburdened themselves to her over the Merlot in the evening and the tea in the morning. She liked hearing her language spoken by people for whom it was baffling and incomplete. They had drawn together. The attraction for her wasn't so much the sex as the lying side by side,

53

touching and examining a skin that was not her own. She would trace the constellations of their moles and invent names for the discoveries: the archer, the fish, the vine. She would ruffle the dark stalks of body hair like a breeze in a cornfield, delighting in the springiness of their growth. Her nose would seek out the particular smells of underarm and neck, teasing out the human from the soap and shampoo. This was like a feast for her.

Her mind glanced against the more off-than-on affair with a peripatetic librarian that she had had after moving back to Mayham. Necessity (his wife and her mother) had meant that his car was where they encountered each other. She had rather liked the seedy aspect of it, but the discomfort drained the pleasure eventually. Besides, she had never been convinced that he smelt right.

Four lovers in a lifetime. She counted them and ranked them, and, lying in her bed while Jozef was making his own discoveries on the other side of the wall, she wondered whether they thought of her now. She drifted to nothingness, but that night she dreamt of lying next to a naked Jozef while he slept, wanting to touch his creamy skin but not daring to wake him.

She got up early the next day, a bit uncomfortable for having intruded on Jozef in her dreams. As softly as she could, she padded down the stairs so as not to disturb the pair. She imagined them resting, curled pinkly together in Jozef's single bed in the sparse whitewashed room. She closed the kitchen door and made her tea and toast as though there was a toddler napping in the next room. That done, she went straight out into the spring garden to give Jozef the space to lounge with or usher out his lover without stumbling over her. Still somewhat disturbed by the voluptuousness of her dreaming world, she made her daily visit to the greenhouse. This morning she saw to her delight that fragile hooks of whitish green had pushed aside crumbs of the moist compost to find the light.

Coming up for light

Monica felt the creeping joy of rising sap as April arrived. As the weather warmed, Monica sowed in the garden too: leeks, carrots, beetroot, parsnips. Some of the seedlings from the greenhouse were destined for the garden and, brought on by the added warmth and shelter she had given them, were by mid-April ready to plant out. The greenhouse project had been a success and the weather had supplied the necessary amount of rain and enough sun to give her outside plants a good start. Soon she would be able to drop some shopping visits to town as the rhubarb, broad beans and spinach that had over wintered were nearly ready to harvest.

In the greenhouse, some seeds came up and some didn't. Those that didn't, she re-sowed a couple of weeks later. Weeds came up. Monica pulled them from the soil with finger and thumb, delicately extricating them from between the seedlings she did want, patting down the disrupted soil.

It was while moving trays of lettuce seedlings out to the garden one fine morning, that Monica noticed a fat loop of a stem had emerged in one of the emulsion tins under the yoghurt seed pots. It was a volunteer; she had not yet planted that container up. It was clearly some kind of cucurbit; it was most likely from one of the pumpkins she grew last year. They were tough seeds and often survived the fiery trials of the heap. Normally she pulled these out. The offspring of these most monstrous of vegetable fruits were unreliable as they crossbred promiscuously. However, there was something in the jizz of this one that made her hesitate. She left it to grow on for the moment and got on with her pleasant task of transplanting the floppy red lettuces to their new bed.

From the neighbourhood came the sounds of children playing outside in the warming weather, and the first whine of lawnmowers.

Jozef was keen on the cook and the cook liked him; he came to stay several times a week, slipping in and out like a thief.

Each day, Monica began her garden rounds in the greenhouse. She always looked first at the volunteer pumpkin plant. She had carefully uprooted it from the tub and set it in a good size yoghurt pot to be transferred to the garden once the frosts had safely passed. It was a fast grower. The hook of the emerging stalk had lengthened and then pulled up from the soil pale twin leaves, the tips bound together by the flat oval seed case from which they had grown. Monica eased it off so the leaves could separate. The next day she found the leaves had opened and were roughly horizontal, leaning slightly to the sun on a thickening stalk. Curiously, the thin veins were tinged with pink. Her instinct had been right, she felt. This was evidently an unusual form, some kind of hybrid or possibly a mutation, worth keeping for curiosity's sake. She felt she had enough room in her garden to admit a few oddities.

Flourishing

The unusual plant that had piqued her curiosity soon needed transplanting again. It was surely some kind of pumpkin to be so vigorous. The pair of oval leaves that it had used to establish its connection with the energy of the sun had been superseded by its true leaves. These were raggedly heart-shaped and faintly bristly. They had hydraulically unfolded their early crinkles like a butterfly's wings emerging from a chrysalis. Already the growing tip showed signs of another pair of larger leaves on the way. It looked like it was going to need a lot of space.

Monica prepared a bed for it near the house so that it could spread its fruiting tendrils across the sunny patio. At the beginning of May, she slotted the sturdy little plant into a hole in the middle of its own bed enriched with three bucketfuls of compost. She back-filled with the compost and then pressed it down firmly to ensure that the fragile, white, hairy roots, that had already crept down the sides of the pot, would soon find the nutrients they were groping for. She slowly poured a whole watering can of water on the soil around it. The soil particles were washed down and resettled themselves next to the root hair cells. The minerals could again be pumped in and transported along the xylem to the solar-powered factories of leaf cells. This done, she went to have a cup of tea and put her feet up for five minutes.

The plant paused; it was a little shocked by the unpotting. The constraints that had defined the under half of the world for it were no longer there. But, by molecular clockwork, life went on. Eased by the water, the growing tips of the roots, tender and pale, probed for new resources to feed on. Thanks to Monica's magical compost they found them in delightful abundance. Up top, there was confusion and consternation in the leaf department. Air was rushing around it in a way it had never experienced before and rocked its stem. Well, it would just have to grow a stronger one. And the wind pulled the water out of its pores so fast it thought it would faint. But down below water was already being passed cell to cell in a microscopic chain to replace the losses above. The sun felt beautifully strong, but later in the dark time, the cold was so intense that the plant slipped into unconsciousness until the faint light of morning revived it.

The plant barely grew in that first week, as far as Monica could see, and it flopped around a bit in the breeze, but it did not die. All the growth was going on underground, the logistics of supply being established before the growth above could advance. By the end of a week though, it was ready for action.

You will know how the next bit goes. Basically, the plant got bigger and bigger and bigger.

A Couple of Kids

The house next door to Monica was occupied by a nice modern family called the Brown-Joneses. They were modern in the sense of being two broken homes patched together into a new one. Mr Jones had Jad and Mrs Brown had Beth and together they had Michael. Jad and Beth rubbed along pretty well given that they hadn't had much choice in the matter. Jad was nine, a tall, blond boy with glasses. He was both robust and imaginative, much in demand in the playground. He would invent and star in complex games that just about anybody who wanted to could join in with. Beth was a year younger. She was a quiet girl, a watcher at heart, but quite capable of holding her own with Jad. She had wide blue eyes, freckles and brown hair drawn loosely into two long plaits. When the weather was fine, they would spend many hours in their garden inventing situations and declaring their changing roles.

When Michael was born, they both drew together in conspiratorial disdain for the new arrival and the disruption and noise he caused. As it became clear that something was wrong with Michael, their hearts did not warm to him much, but they were careful to share their thoughts with each other rather than the wider family. The extra care that Mr Jones and Mrs Brown had to give to the flesh of their conjoined flesh, was set to last and Michael wasn't shaping up anytime soon to be much use for anything at all. By the time he was two, you would notice that his face looked a bit odd and his little arms and legs were too feeble to allow him to move around on his own. Sometimes Jad and Beth would play peek-a-boo with him or try to make him smile by clapping or baby-talking to him. The results, however, were rather unsatisfactory, so they didn't make a habit of it except when their parents or their other relatives were there to applaud their efforts.

The adult Brown-Joneses were too wrapped up in the grown-up business of putting food on the table and caring for little Michael to notice much of what was happening next door, but Jad and Beth were keen observers.

They saw Monica weeding and planting, but often she would just stroke the plants or stand still for a long time just looking at her garden. They watched her pick off caterpillars and snails and squish them underfoot. From time to time, they would lie on their stomachs on the scratchy grass to look through the gaps at the base of the privet hedge that separated their house from the one next door and speculate about the weird woman who lived next door.

She was ideal witch material to two junior school children. In the first place, she lived alone, as far as they could tell (no cat, but they dismissed that as a ploy to keep her being a witch from being detected). Secondly, there was the garden. They had watched her dig up her lawn and seen her tend and harvest her plants as though it was all she had to do. Her clothes were baggy and ugly, and her thick, black hair hung down shaggily over her shoulders. They guessed she was smelly though they had never been close enough to test this out. Once they saw a snake slither out from under the cover of the compost heap when Monica lifted it up. She had just watched it and smiled. They had whispered debates about whether she was a good witch or a bad witch, both rather hoping that she was bad.

As the weather warmed enough for Monica to plant out pumpkins without fear of frost, the children inhabited the garden more and more. Left to themselves while their parents were busy with Michael or something else, they hatched daring plots to find solid proof of her witchiness that they could reveal to their small world of close friends. Weeks of discussion of possible forays into next door's garden to gather evidence took their toll on the two children. At length, they were at bursting point with daring but frozen with fear of a real-world encounter. Something had to happen and so happen it did.

It was a hot, windless day in the Whitsun half-term. They were sucking on homemade orange juice ice lollies, lying on their backs in the shade of the privet. They watched the clouds make fluffy crocodiles and elongated rhinos.

"Look Beth, that one's a witch. Look, you can see the broomstick with the cat on." He pointed upwards with the dripping remains of his lolly.

"Where? I can't see it."

"Over there, you silly, just by the block of flats."

"That's not a witch! That's a dragon. Look, you can see the flames coming out of its mouth."

"It doesn't look a bit like a dragon unless it's a dragon that's exploded and then been put together all wrong. It's a witch; look you can see the pointy hat and everything." He sucked the last piece of lolly off his stick and crunched it.

"Well, I can't see it. And I'm not a silly, you are. And besides, not all witches have pointy hats. *She* doesn't."

Jad turned away from considering the sky and looked squarely at Beth. "Well, I don't think she is a witch. She's probably just someone's gran. We've never seen her doing anything properly witchy," Jad pointed out.

Beth rolled onto her side to face him. "She wouldn't do anything witchy out here in the daytime would she? Witches would do all their spells at night time, wouldn't they? I bet she does them when it's a full moon. That's when we'd catch her at it."

"All right then, we'll sneak out when it's full moon and see what she gets up to."

"You wouldn't dare!" gasped Beth.

"I would! You're the one who's a scaredy cat."

"I am not! You're always the one who chickens out of things."

"Well, I won't chicken out of this one," Jad concluded firmly.

Jad scrambled to his feet and ran into the kitchen, followed by Beth, lolly sticks abandoned on the grass. They found their mum sitting at the table playing Candy Crush on her phone. Casually, Jad asked when there would next be a full moon. Mrs Brown-Jones was gratified to have such enquiring and scientifically-minded children and so looked up the phases of the moon on her phone there and then. Discovering there was to be one this very night, they lost all interest in astronomy and ran back out to the garden to make their plan.

The Night Garden

After dinner, Mr and Mrs Brown-Jones were pleasantly surprised by how meekly the children went off to bed and spent a quiet evening together watching telly. While the ten o'clock news told them of fresh atrocities, scandalous neglect and the usual political bickering, their children crept downstairs and out the back door to the orangey darkness of their suburban garden.

A garden at night is quite a different beast from its daylight form. The patio is more uneven, the grass damp and black, and the flowers mere grey shadows of the colourful splashes that they make by day. Both the children were hushed by the loss of familiarity and had no need to shush each other. Instinctively they reached out and held hands as they made their halting way to their usual vantage point by the hedge. It was cool in the night breeze and they hesitated to lie on the grass amongst the unseen creepy crawlies. Instead, they stood close to the hedge, covered in darkness, and peered into Monica's garden. The whitewashed wall of the house was easy to see and light seeped out around the curtains of a downstairs room revealing the lean-to greenhouse and the patio crowded with pots. A sweet smell from some scented bush with insignificant flowers caught their attention and made them inhale more deeply. The quiet hum of traffic from the main road brushed the scene with a thin layer of distant sound. As they tuned into the quietness, they heard the muted noise of the television from their own house where their parents sat in contented ignorance of their adventure. In next door's garden there was nothing to see in the way of cauldrons and spell books. They stood, disappointed and relieved until they began to feel chilly in their thin cartoon pyjamas.

"Let's go in," Beth said, "I'm cold."

"All right then, if you want," replied Jad, relieved not to be the first to suggest it.

More deftly now that their eyes had adjusted to the dark, they turned and made their way to the back door. Quietly, Jad turned the handle and pushed. It didn't open. He tried again, as noiselessly as he could, but with more force. Nothing happened. Jad felt tears rise to his eyes as his clever scheme tumbled into humiliation and fear.

"Come on, Jad; it's really cold. I want to go to bed," whispered Beth.

Jad had another go with the door but with no success. He turned to his sister and said, "They must have gone to bed and locked it." Beth opened her mouth and eyes wide but said nothing. What was there to say?

"Shall I just knock?" he said. Beth looked more scared and shook her head rapidly.

Jad struggled to think how he could make things all right. "Let's have a look and see if there's a window open. Come on, Beth."

Voicelessly, they made their way in their slippers down the sideway and round to the front of the house. All the windows on the ground floor were shut, but their bedroom casement was a little way open. Jad gazed at it critically. He was a good climber, but he couldn't see a way he could do it. He wondered if they could sleep out and then get up really early and sneak in when their parents had gotten up and unlocked the door. Beth was hugging herself and looking at him.

"Look, let's knock, Beth; they won't be angry," but he knew it was a lie and so did she. It was exactly the kind of thing that would make their parents really angry. Beth was mute in her anxiety and just shook her head again.

The noise of a door opening startled both of them. Next door, the woman who might be a witch was coming out of her front door carrying a recycling crate. She walked up the short path and fumbled open the wooden garden gate while balancing the crate on her knee. She set down the box on the pavement and turned to go back in. Without thinking much beyond the sudden chance of a solution to the mess he had got himself and Beth into, Jad spoke up.

"Excuse me? Could you help us?" Once said, this could not be unsaid and things that would not otherwise happen were now bound to occur.

"Oh! You made me jump!" She put a hand to her chest but smiled.

"Sorry, we didn't mean to," Jad gabbled.

"Oh no. Don't worry about that. Hello. What are you two doing out here?" She looked at them intently, taking in the nightwear, the pale worried faces, the hands holding and being held.

Jad explained their situation. He left out the bit about spying on her to see if she was a witch and cleverly, he judged, substituted a vague quest concerning something important that they'd lost in the garden. He didn't say what he wanted her to do to help; he just felt relieved that there was some sort of known adult he could turn to that wasn't an angry parent. It didn't seem at all likely that she was a witch now. He could feel Beth's hand gripping his more tightly though, so he turned to her.

"Beth, it'll be fine. The nice lady will help us."

The lady considered them and said, "I think the best thing really is for you to knock on the door and get your parents to let you in. You can't stay out here in the garden all night, can you?"

Jad's face fell. This was no solution at all. "But they'll be really angry. I know they will."

"That's as maybe," she said briskly, "but really what else can you do?"

"Can't you help us sneak in? Look, the window's open up there," Jad said desperately, knowing full well that sneaking like that was not the kind of thing that old women like her did.

She looked at Jad, frowning a little. "Hmm. Well, I have got a ladder. I suppose you could use that if you really wanted to."

"Yes, yes! Please." Jad felt a surge of elation as a way out of his trouble miraculously came into being.

The lady went round the side of her house and returned a few minutes later with a shiny metal ladder. She crossed from her garden to theirs via the pavement and the two matching garden gates. She set the ladder against the wall under the bedroom window. It was way too short. Then she lifted the top section and, with a tinny squeak, it grew up like a beanstalk to touch and then pass the windowsill. She took a step to the side and held the upright edge. She nodded to Jad to go up.

Jad put his hands on the cold metal and began to climb. When he had got a few steps up, he turned to Beth.

"You come up when I get through the window," he whispered. Steadfastly mute, Beth nodded and looked a little dubiously at the woman. The woman offered a smile, but Beth, unconvinced, didn't return it.

Jad climbed slowly to the top then clambered over the sill. He mouthed at Beth to come on, and she too started the clandestine ascent to safety. She focussed on the window, not wanting to see the ground retreat below her; all her courage was screwed up for the climb and she knew she had none to spare for the possibility of falling. Up she went, two furry pink-slippered feet on each rung before attempting the next. The night breeze blew in sharp little gusts around her making her feel cold and exposed. Eventually, she reached the window where Jad was waiting to help her in. She scrambled awkwardly over the sill and then she stood at last in the safe carpeted interior of their bedroom. She relaxed and allowed herself a little gasp of relief. Jad grinned. They both went over to the window and gave a thumbs up to the woman down below. She raised her hand in acknowledgement and, with a final few squeals, collapsed the ladder and carried it through her gate and round the side to her own back garden. The children watched from the window to see if she would reappear, but she was gone.

When Jad woke up the next day, safe and undetected, the events of the previous night seemed like a nightmare, terrible but not quite real. He sat up in bed and looked about him. There on the carpet were unmistakeable flecks of dirt leading from the window to the slippers by his bed. Jad tiptoed downstairs to get a dustpan and brush to sweep away the evidence. He felt a peculiar pride in having successfully concealed their exploit from his parents, but as the day wore on, it bothered him that his parents' omniscience had been found so wanting. He pondered on the deception that they had constructed. It wasn't lying because they hadn't said anything that wasn't true. Still, it felt like lying, just the same.

As for the lady next door, by aiding and abetting them, she had entered into a relationship with them that was different from any they had yet experienced. She was very much a grown-up but she had sided with them in their hour of need against what he now knew was the right thing to have done, to have accepted humiliation and a telling off and knocked on the door. This made her both a trustworthy person and a dubious one. And she knew their secret. Would she tell?

Monica, for her part, was feeling uncomfortable too. She knew she had done no harm and had had no intention of doing any, but she felt that she had broken a law that was so well-established that there was no need to articulate it, let alone write it in a statute book. With uncharacteristic anxiety, she waited for the retribution she felt she was due. Once again, none came.

Progress

Oblivious to all these goings on, the pumpkin plant followed its unique blueprint and month by month moved towards its final goal of reproduction. Monica took notes.

May 17th: A bushy robust plant. Mid-green with an unusual rosy tinge to the veins. Three pairs of leaves, each set larger than the last. Watered copiously. Minor slug damage.

June 10th: Extensive leaf growth. Leaves over a foot across held up on unusually thick prickly stalks. Top growth covers the bed. Looks like it will need more space, but too late to transplant again now. Watered well. No sign of pest damage.

July 2nd: Multiple growing tips developed from centre. Each looks set to be a fruit-bearing stalk.

July 29th: Fruiting stalks now extend two metres across the patio. Repositioned stalks so I don't keep tripping over them. Flowers have developed; (buds up to six inches long). Look like twisted dusters! Plant very healthy.

August 5th: Flowers have started opening and are a reddish-orange and trumpet-shaped with the reproductive organs clearly visible. Hand pollinated with a paintbrush – a bit fiddly but satisfying. Started weekly feeding (diluted wee and liquid from rotted bindweed roots 1:1:10).

August 12th: Some small round fruits swelling behind the flower heads. It looks more like pumpkins than marrows or butternut squash.

August 17th: Counted twelve small fruits this morning. They are just beginning to colour to yellow.

August 23rd: Removed a few pale soft fruits. Looks like these didn't get fertilised. Still around seven good-looking ones left.

August 30th: Something weird happening. Most of the fruits are looking a bit off, but one of them is growing really fast.

September 8th: Had to compost all but one of the pumpkins. They had started shrivelling and beginning to rot near the stalk. Checked for pest damage, but nothing obvious. Virus? Fungus? Googled, but couldn't find anything. What's going on? Perhaps an internal competition for resources?

September 15th: The single fruit has grown to a good size, about a foot across. The fruit is mid-orange with dark green striping and fairly smooth. No signs of what happened to the other fruits happening here.

October 1st: Fruit hasn't got bigger recently. It's lost its stripes and is now wholly orange. Leaves and stalks are fading and getting brittle. Quite a lot of mildew. Tested rind with fingernail and it felt very hard so should now be good for keeping. Harvested pumpkin.

Monica got out her secateurs and cut the hardened cord that held the bulging fruit on to the now decrepit plant. The fruit was handsome enough, evenly grown, sound and just a little discoloured where it had rested its bulk on the damp ground. She was a little disappointed to have only one decent-sized fruit to show for all her care, though she knew it was always a bit of a risk to let the self-seeded ones grow on. Still, it was a good weight and Monica judged it would keep well, unblemished as it was. Other produce was ripening around her so there was an easy abundance of food. Pumpkin soup in the quiet of winter would be a lovely reminder of the warmth and fertility of this bumper year. So she sat the pumpkin on the cold tiles of her larder floor where it reflected the light warmly and silently.

Pumpkin soup

The sun failed slowly in the usual way as the season progressed; getting up a little later, going to bed a little earlier. Monica did the same. The cold regained its hold as the quiet emptiness of the universe was again revealed; that life is an aberration in the universe was restated and underlined. Things that were alive ceased to be so. The cell walls of the tender nasturtiums were spiked through with ice crystals as the water held within them froze and the leaves browned and withered. They gave off a final pungent whiff of spice as though cut through with a kitchen knife. Other plants, better equipped to survive the frosts, simply slowed their metabolism and lay motionless like toads, breathing shallowly, feeding meagrely.

In the old times, this was the season for pig-killing. Those tubby sausage machines, made fat on overgrown marrows and stale bread, would be led snuffling to the shed. After a short unequal struggle in its dark interior, their blood and guts (and other body parts) would be separated from each other to justify their existence and the extra work they had caused. Monica pondered on how this planned and abrupt end of life would qualify the relationship between pig and pig-keeper. The dog in the kennel, the chickens in the coop, the condemned pig in the sty. She quite fancied having a fat, clever pig. She doubted she could stomach the sausages, but perhaps she could find herself capable of that too after what she had already done. For now, though, the compost heap played the same role as the lowly, lonely pig, turning inedible surplus into food, albeit by a slower mineral route.

November came, bringing the dark and presaging the real cold of winter. There was less in the garden to harvest: only the winter staples of leeks, chard, kale and parsnips. One morning, when the pouring rain made the garden a poor prospect, Monica tied on her apron and fetched the pumpkin from the larder floor. The bad weather had made Monica think of spicy, warm pumpkin soup for lunch. The time was ripe for enjoying the fruits of her summer labour.

Once set on the kitchen table, she inspected it closely. There was no sign of decay but it had made a slightly hollow sound as she had lowered it. A sign that it was properly matured and that the seeds had formed completely. With the weather like this, she would take the time to process the seeds into chewy roast snacks, more mouth toy than food. The hard orange skin felt oddly not quite cold to her fingers as she passed her hands over its form, tracing the smooth parts and the small rough area where it had lain on the earth. Admiring the deep colour of the skin, she sought the right place to make the incision. She always cut her produce along a line of symmetry out of respect. She swivelled it until she found the right place. It was like making the first slice in an elaborately iced birthday cake – it seemed a shame, but, really, unless you did destroy it there was no point to it at all.

In went the little vegetable knife, just beneath the stalk. She pressed it down hard to penetrate the thick skin and cleave the firm flesh below. She followed the line down, pressing steadily, and then rotated the globe to continue up the other side to the stalk again. She squeezed her fingers in the deep, damp cut and prised the two sides apart, now hinged only by the stalk. As the two halves came apart, the stalk popped off like a callous that was no longer needed.

Now that she could see inside, it was plain that all was not as it should be. Instead of the expected flat, oval seeds arranged around a stringy core, there was some kind of sac made of a silky, cream-coloured membrane. Was it a fruit inside a fruit? Like a miniature pale green pepper found nestling immaturely inside a big red one? She prodded it gently with her knife to get the measure of it. There was an answering movement from inside. She felt a wave of revulsion. Was there some kind of maggot infestation in it? A great white ribbed beast that had burrowed inside as a tiny saw-toothed thread and then bulked monstrously as it tunnelled through the nutritious flesh? Or a nest of tiny pale wrigglers ready to spill blindly across her kitchen table as soon as she opened the sac? Perhaps a flimsy cocoon of exotically deadly pumpkin spiders hitherto unknown in the UK? She had to see but didn't much fancy her kitchen full of exotic pests.

After a moment's thought, she decided that she would have a proper look at it on the back porch with the kitchen door shut. The garden would have been better, but the rain continued to collide noisily with the window. She got her phone and took a picture of the now motionless sac lying in the half hollow of the pumpkin. She took a few more from different angles. Taking care not to disturb it, she lifted it off the table. Holding it as far from her body as the weight allowed, she carried it out to the back porch. She set it on the ground, looking all the time for signs of life. Nothing. She went to the kitchen and got the knife and a plastic tub with a lid for whatever was inside. She slipped her phone into her pocket. Lastly, she got some blue latex gloves that she kept for clearing the drains and closed the kitchen door firmly behind her

She felt like a surgeon all gloved up as she got down on her garden kneeling mat on the cold tiled floor of the porch. Making herself as comfortable as she could in the cramped space, she made a tiny cut in the sac. It was pliable and slightly waxy. The knife cut through it easily. To her relief, nothing poured out. Nothing even moved. Had she imagined the movement before? She must have done. It was certainly the most likely thing. Instantly, she felt a red wave of foolishness as she knelt in the cold porch, and glanced up to the people who might be standing behind her, watching her. No witnesses to her idiocy were there, thank goodness. She exhaled a puff of tense air and settled herself. She cut the sac again, more boldly. There was definitely something in there and it didn't look like seeds. More like the giant maggot theory, but not quite that either. She cut a little more and there it was again, a movement from inside. She sat back on her heels, exhaling heavily. Another picture with the camera, although there was nothing really that could be seen for sure in the shrouded interior of the sac under the clouded November sky. She wondered if she should call someone, but Jozef was already at work and calling the children next door would not be right at a time like this. Whatever this time was.

Biting her bottom lip, she continued cutting until she had slit the sac from top to bottom. She paused, consciously taking deep breaths to calm herself. She readied herself to pull the sides apart and peer inside. Blue finger and thumb on each smooth side she opened up the sac. Inside was a creature. Not vegetable, but animal. It squirmed a bit at the intrusion of air or light. It was curled on its side and was a creamy whitish colour. Definitely not a maggot as it had a head and limbs. No, not limbs: arms and legs.

It was about six inches long. It looked like a minute, skinny person. It had a face: a flattish one with a turned up nose like a baby. Its mouth was closed and lipless. Its eyes too were closed. Something was missing… It had no ears, just smooth skin where they should have been. It was hairless. There was a rhythmic movement about it; it was breathing. It was at the same time both appealing and abhorrent. Did she dare touch it? What else was she to do? She thought of taking a picture, but somehow this did not feel like the right thing to do. Why was that?

The thing didn't look rotten or noxious or dangerous. She couldn't just put it on the compost heap or chop it up and add it to the soup. So she put her gloved finger lightly on its exposed side. It squirmed in reaction making her jump and pull her hand away. What was she to do now? She stood up and looked at it. It didn't move. She put her hand back in and prodded it gently again and this time she did not jump when it moved. She pressed it a little – it was firm and it squirmed away. Its skin was smooth and cool; she felt no human warmth through the glove. It made no noise.

What was she to do? What was the right thing? What was the best thing? Like shutting a door to the room full of monsters in a nightmare, she felt an urge to close the pumpkin back around it and leave it somewhere. Somewhere in the garden? Would it suffocate inside now that she had opened it? Had she broken some umbilical bond in cutting the fruit that meant there was now no backwards, only forwards to life or death? Like the telltale heart of Poe's murderer would she always hear faint scratching when the house was quiet as it clawed uselessly at the hard orange flesh with its tiny fingers? Did it have fingernails? She hadn't seen. All the memories of Monica's earlier murder landed on her fresh and raw: the terrible slow noisy breaths of her exhausting, expiring mother; the sleepless night of terror and inaction; the silent morning at the intersection of familiarity and horror. Was this some kind of retribution by reincarnation? The pit of her stomach rolled and Monica was stricken.

She sat back. She had no stomach for killing this thing, even by neglect, even though it could so easily have died without her intervention by rotting in *Cucurbita pepo* on her larder floor. She gave her head a shake to distract herself from that disturbing thought and peered again into the sac. The creature had changed position and was lying on its back and moving its arms weakly in an aimless sort of way. It really was astonishing that such a thing had come to be. Unbelievable. She took off her gloves and pressed her damp face with her hands to see if she was dreaming. It didn't feel like a dream. The air was too cool, the curtain of rain too three dimensional and the thud of blood in her ears too visceral for her to fail to credit the evidence of her senses.

What was she to do? This was the ultimate scientific curiosity, worthy of the finest Victorian cabinet, along with the wizened stitched mermaids and the twin-legged mandrake roots. Should it be pickled like an onion or a two-headed calf? No, no! Should it be dissected? No. But surely it was worthy of study. It deserved a place in history, the cover of the New Scientist, a headline on the News at Ten. She'd mostly stopped listening to the news, sick of the spectacle of failure, hatred and vanity. She shuddered as she considered the reporters wanting a story: coming up to the door, knocking, not going away, taking photographs of her hurrying away head down, tight-lipped. The scientists too would want to know everything. Where it came from, how it came to be there, the raw ingredients of death and life that had been reshaped in her garden into this new kind of life. The whole world would want to know. Naturally, they would want to know and knowing this how could she reasonably refuse? Her entire life would be thrown open and picked over by the hungry press and diligent scientists. She couldn't face that.

With nothing else to do, she gazed at it. It was so helpless, like an unwanted kitten, blind and defenceless. Its humanish form made it look naked as though it required clothes to be provided for it. Yet it was undeniably monstrous too with its subtle aberrations from the human form. To not kill the thing demanded positive action; to leave it and do nothing was murderous, a crime of infanticide by the wilderness of the garden: hypothermia, dehydration, predation. Could she, should she stamp on it like a snail, exposing its undoubtedly unique tubular innards? She pictured them blue and twisted with white lobes of unknowable function. She could claim it as something that had never really happened, like a teenage termination put well behind you as you forge onwards with your planned career. Monica knew she had stepped beyond the bounds of textbook, law-book ethics when she had taken her mother's life in her own hands and stood self-aware at the centre of her own shifting moral universe. It was all down to her.

The combination of vegetable and human attributes mathematically averaged out to an animal-like status. Was this a pet then? Or vermin? Like a stray from a brood of wrinkly rat pups incubated in the foetid heat of the compost heap?

It squirmed a little more, still noiseless. Was the autumn air cooling its pale skin? Reluctant to hold it in her hands but wanting instinctively to assuage its apparent discomfort, she hunted out something to pick it up with. She found a soft, clean amber duster and gently eased the cloth around the little body. In doing so she discovered with a jolt that there was a pliable vine-like structure extending from its belly to a dark patch hidden under it on the hollow of the pumpkin below. As she manoeuvred the cloth around to encase the pumpkin child, it broke off like the stalk of a ripe apple from its parent branch. She had definitely gone and done it now.

Next door, the children had just got in from school, tired out in that particular frenetic, noisy, hungry way. A new school year had begun, with new teachers, new projects and new clubs. This term it was to be Drama Club on Wednesdays for Beth and Minecraft on Thursdays for Jad.

Jozef was looking at the clock at work, impatient to be on his way home, hoping to sleep for an hour or two between his shifts.

The unusual pumpkin plant that had succoured this extraordinary creature was expiring without pain, chopped into rough pieces, melting into its component parts on the heap. As it gently lost its integrity, it drifted peaceably across the boundary from something into nothing.

Monica was sitting on her bed weeping gently while the pumpkin child stretched and wriggled, pushing at its duster bedclothes. It had been shielded from the horrors of both abandonment and vivisection and lay in a shoe box by her side.

Trial and Error

Monica made no decision that day. She had acted without making decisions when she had lifted up the pumpkin child and swaddled it and stowed it in the box. She just looked and looked at it, absorbing the reality of it, adjusting her inner world to one that included such a departure from what you would reasonably expect life to throw at you. She took it to her room and stayed there with it for the rest of the day, growing a little more used to it all the time. Each time she left the room, to get a drink or go to the toilet, the reality of it would diminish as soon as it was out of sight, like a dream in the waking world. She hesitated each time she returned to the room before opening the door, uncertain of what she would see in the shoebox on the bed. Without fail, there it was, alive and unbelievable.

Monica gazed at it. This is what she saw. A six-inch long homunculus, with the body proportions of a slim toddler. Pale skin, like the albino child who had been in the year below her at school. The hands had thumbs but only three fingers and no fingernails. This gave it the appearance of a cartoon character, anthropomorphic but smooth and easy to draw. Its feet likewise had no toenails but had six toes and a protrusion at the back of each tiny heel like another nail-less toe but longer and more curved. It had no hair as far as she could tell. And where its legs joined its body there were no tiny sex organs, only a pinhole of an anus. Would it need nappies? Where the cord that connected it to the pumpkin had broken off, there was a little protrusion, a belly bump that was brownish. The face was human-like, with the small mouth and nose and big eyes (still closed) of a young child. The eyes remained shut all day. Would they open? She wondered if the eyes had not formed properly and it would remain in the dark. Perhaps it had no soul that needed windows.

When she heard the door open as Jozef returned home from his first shift, her heart hammered with fear and guilt. Her gut, or some part of her reptile brain, wanted to keep this secret, so she laid low, feigning absence, glad the thing was apparently unable to cry out or indeed make any vocalisations. All that day the rain continued, grey and heavy, cooling the air and adding to Monica's sense of claustrophobia and isolation. The dark came early, the heavy cloud masking the weakening light from the low autumn sun. Dinnerless, she lay on the bed in the gloom, dozing, listening to the tiny hamsterish movements from the box beside her. After a while she felt thoroughly chilled and, without getting undressed, shifted herself under the duvet, making sure the box was half under too and safe from toppling over in the night.

She dreamt of being transferred to a new library, but not being able to understand the instructions of where it was or what she was meant to do when she got there. It was a modern building and had several floors. She found herself walking around it with growing anxiety, trying to understand how the books were arranged. It made no sense to her although there was clearly some kind of system from the labels and signs that she was unable to decipher. The carpet was a vivid blue.

She woke alert and anxious with a sense that she had forgotten to do something vitally important. It was not quite light, but it felt like morning was close. All was quiet. Was that right? She felt for the shoebox. It was there in the bed next to her. She hesitated to put her hand in it in the dark, but she had to have a look in. She fumbled with the bedside light. Then, there it was, whatever it was. It was quite still. Sleeping? Dead? She prodded it gently with a fingertip. It moved its pale arm a little, but not much. Something was wrong. What was it? Was it ill? It didn't look quite right. Again she gave it a gentle poke, a little harder this time. Again it moved weakly in response. It seemed too floppy, wilted almost, like her mother's houseplants when her neglect had begun to show. Water! Obviously, it needed water. Everything that was alive needed water and whatever else it was, it was alive. The fact of it coming into life was not enough, it must stay alive. All that empty-headed looking yesterday had, without her meaning it to, forged a bond, a bond maternal enough for her care to be assured.

She rolled out of bed and pulled on her dressing gown. She must get it some water straight away. Creeping down the narrow stairs so as not to rouse Jozef, she fetched a cup of water from the kitchen. Gingerly, and not without a thrill of disgust in her work, she gathered up the little thing in the duster. It was weak and flaccid compared with yesterday. She propped it in her lap and for lack of a better plan or a Dr Spock guide to caring for mutant plant offspring, dipped her finger in the water and dabbed it on the lipless mouth. It reacted instantly and made Monica start as a tiny, purple, tubular tongue flicked out and greedily sucked the drips from her finger. It felt like a minute feather-light vacuum cleaner hoovering up the moisture. When her finger was dry, the tongue rolled back up and into the mouth. She dipped her finger again, and again it unrolled its tongue, more like a butterfly's proboscis than anything human, and sucked up the water. It had quite a thirst. Monica found the strange tickly sensation pleasant enough once she had overcome her shock at its anatomy. It made her smile.

Eventually, it had had enough and lost interest in the offered drips. Monica felt relief that she had overcome a hurdle and sat back on the bed leaning against the wall, the pumpkin child resting on her lap. She dozed, half-dreaming of two-headed lambs, giant marrows and naked, squirming, blind, baby rats.

The sun climbed and when she opened her eyes again morning, as well as the strange creature, was indubitable. Food then. What would it eat? Sunlight or Farley's rusks? She pictured the feeding tube probing the hard, dusty surface of a rusk like an elephant at a crazed, dried-up waterhole and decided against that. Glucose would be a safer bet, a common denominator for plants and animals. She had white sugar for jam-making. Would that do? It was worth a go. The pumpkin child was sleeping now, so she lifted it off her lap and propped it up in the warmish hollow of the pillow where her back had rested and went down to the kitchen.

The kitchen appeared comically normal considering what had happened yesterday. She gazed around at the stack of pans on the shelf, the washing up on the draining board, the pedal bin whose plastic pedal had broken off but that still basically worked. She sat down heavily in the wooden chair at the table and rubbed her face hard to remind herself of what real was.

After a minute or so, she pulled herself up and put the kettle on. She made herself a cup of tea. In the cupboard she noticed a thin china teacup decorated with cornflowers. Perhaps that would do. She put a teaspoon of sugar in it then poured in some water from the kettle. She sipped it. Too hot. Too strong. She topped it up with water from the tap, tasted it again and was satisfied. Treading quietly, she climbed the stairs back to her room and to her charge. It was still sleeping. She drank her hot tea sat on the end of her bed dividing her gaze between the creature and the view out the window of her wet and withering garden. There were things in the garden that needed doing: cutting back, tying up, mulching. Yet she looked on the brownness of it unmoved and unmoving. On her bed, the pumpkin child shifted its weight and feebly slumped over onto its side waving its limbs as though to right itself. She got up and went over to it. Its face was still and blank like a mask. Perhaps it had feelings but just no way of showing them, at least as yet. Tentatively she lifted it up and rested it on her lap, leaning its side against her belly and keeping her hand supporting its back so it didn't fall backwards. She reached across for the cup on the table next to her bed. She touched it to its mouth, tipping it so the liquid came into contact with its lips. The feeding tube instantly rolled out and started to suck up the sweet liquid. She watched it fascinated, nipples tingling. A little while later, it rolled up its tongue, apparently satisfied. It shifted from side to side, gave a tiny belch, and opened its eyes.

Something Familiar

The eyes shut again. Then they opened again and blinked slowly several times. The eyes were black slits between the pale hairless lids. It kept blinking as though the dim light was painful, but, as the seconds ticked on, it opened them more and more widely. Apart from a triangle of white in each corner, the eyes were completely black. It moved its head in feeble jerks from side to side. Could it see her? There was no sign that it marked the pattern of light and shade that made up her face and body any more than it noticed the pastel stripes and flowers on the duvet cover. It could see though; that much was clear from the movement of its bald head as it looked around with bird-like twitches. She felt a ripple of fear. It conveyed the impression less of a creature that was entirely vulnerable and more like a being with the potential for agency. She sat completely frozen, like a fearful rabbit.

In time, the head stopped moving and the eyes closed again. She felt the little body relax into sleep. Wanting to get away, she lifted it off her numb leg and, with infinite care not to wake it, stood up and placed it once more against the pillow.

This was too much. To care for a being that manifestly required it she could manage, but she now felt the perceived amorality of the creature to be a danger to herself. She suspected it of malevolence. Was it a familiar come unbidden to torment her for her sins? How could that be? But how could any of this be? A rush of panic swept over her. She had to get away. Without a thought for the poor little thing, she pulled on some clothes and stepped out the room, closing the door noiselessly after her. She slipped down the stairs, put on her coat and boots and left the house.

Once on the pavement, she instinctively turned away from town and started walking. She walked and walked. She found herself along the A road that led to other places, letting the dirty smell and thrum of the rush hour traffic displace her careering thoughts. The sky was thin and grey, the air damp. She walked on, as fast as she could. Soon her breath was coming in little puffs and she got too warm in her coat. Sweating and breathless, she strode on welcoming the discomforts of her ageing body. Whenever she started to think of the creature lying asleep or worse, open-eyed on her bed, she la la-ed the image away and walked faster. She got to a roundabout, exits labelled clearly to other towns, near and far. How far could she walk? To be somewhere else would be an adventure. She had never really travelled as much as she'd wanted to. Why not just keep going? She crossed the first feeder road badly. She was beeped by an indignant van driver who opened his window to swear at her, leaving her speechless and shamed. She crossed the other roads more carefully until she ended up on the road she had come in on but on the opposite side. She walked back home, slowly, sweat cooling in chilly, smelly stains on her greyish vest.

*

Monica opened her front door and stepped in. She undid her coat, shrugged it off and hung it over a chair in the kitchen. The kitchen contrived to look innocent. More tea. A piece of toast from the drying end of a dense home-baked loaf. Red jam from some bush or other in the garden. Bite, chew, slurp, exhale. Another slice of toast to help weigh her down to the stuff of the world. The stickiness of the jam, the crumbliness of the toast and the steam of the tea all helped her. At last, feeling more solid, she climbed the stairs to begin again. A new leaf.

The faded pillowcase nest was bare. Where was it? Had it got out? Had it faded in the morning light like the ancient scam of fairy gold? Had next door's cat got it? Its presence had been a problem, but now so was its absence. She scanned the untidy bedclothes for signs of it. For signs that it had ever been there. She was sure it had; the intensity of the memory was undeniable. Either she had completely lost her grip on reality, or it had been here and now it wasn't. Where was it? She feared its discovery more than its death since she had so inexplicably hidden it away. She would deny everything. She had never seen it before. Where was it?

As she was rehearsing her lines, she saw it on the floor, using its tiny limbs to somehow move itself along like a sloth crossing a motorway. It must have tumbled out of the bed and onto the cold, hard floorboards. Swiftly, she stooped to pick it up, feeling its smooth cool flesh without a shudder. There was no sign of injury. Its eyes were open. She looked at it. It seemed to look back at her. Maybe the movement of her body had caught its attention and by some vestigial human trait it latched on to her face and eyes. Its gaze was steady and unsmiling. They looked at each other, human and not. She smiled and then gave a quick laugh for the strangeness and adventure of it.

She resolved at that moment to just get on with it, with a life of which this creature was a part for the moment at least. The last couple of days of being shut in were enough for her. She needed to find a way to keep the pumpkin child safe and alive (happy?) while she went about her life. She had used a sling to carry Kate around with her as a baby and had enjoyed at times the hot, fleshy burden of her little body, legs splayed and dangling. In winter, it had been a bit like being heavily pregnant again, her winter coat making a second furry skin. She would make a mini-sling and tuck the little mite in. Looking through the rag bag under the sink she came up with some old T-shirts which were clean and soft. She cut and pinned and sewed for an hour or so until she had made a little carrier with leg holes and soft straps that she could pull over her shoulders so the pouch hung comfortably nestling beneath her large breasts. While she sewed in her room, she glanced from time to time at the creature, now dozing again in her space in the bed. When it voicelessly stirred, she would offer it water or sugar solution and it would suck, eyes closed. Sometimes it wanted neither and would just move its tiny pale head round, resting its gaze on this and that. Other times it would stretch and wave its limbs, sometimes flopping over to the side and then trying to right itself.

The toilet flushed. Jozef was up. There was no reason for him to come into her room, but even so, she pushed a chair against the door. She traced his habitual movements from the sounds that filtered through the walls. When she heard the front door close, she felt her shoulders drop with relief.

By lunchtime the sling was ready. She pulled the straps on over her shoulders then gingerly lifted the pumpkin child up and poked it gently into the pouch, arranging the limbs so it would be comfortable. The pouch was a little too large; she caught herself thinking that it would grow into it. The weight was negligible, far less than the standard bag of sugar. It wriggled a bit but eventually settled, hidden inside except for two spindly legs poking out the sides. She put a big winter fleece over the top and zipped it most of the way up. Looking in the mirror, there was nothing to see as the pouch sheltered in the underhang of her bosom. Holding a monstrous little secret so tidily under her sensible clothing gave her a wave of illicit joy.

The short, grey afternoon of a late November day was just beginning. She left her room and went cautiously downstairs, conscious of her extra new responsibility. In the hallway, she pulled on her old coat and woolly hat and headed out into the garden to see what was happening out there.

A Quick Dip

In this way, Monica resumed her life, tending the garden, making do, going shopping, sitting by the fire, dreaming. Under the surface of her pilled fleece or curled up next to her in bed, the pumpkin child accompanied her silently, basking in the warmth of her fleshy torso. Jozef found her quieter and more self-absorbed than ever, but didn't comment or mind; his own life was rolling on with its own dramas of love and frustrated ambition.

Monica experimented with feeding the thing. It had no teeth as far as she could see, so she mashed and sieved tiny amounts of food through a tea strainer to make thin soups and fruit drinks. When these were presented in the cornflower cup it would flare its nostrils with interest and then unroll its tongue to taste. Pumpkin puree was a favourite, though Monica herself now had some aversion to cooking with them. Each time she took one down from the shelf, she would put her ear to it for a long while and then, with much hesitation, cut it open bit by bit and peer and then poke inside. So far there had been no further surprises.

Once she started feeding it these solid-based foods, she found that it would let pass a small, brownish, dribbly poo once a day or so. It wasn't much effort to clean up. She found that a folded pad of toilet paper placed in the bottom of the sling absorbed the soft mess. One of many little oddities was that it didn't wee; it would sweat but no tinkles. Thank heavens for that.

After about a week, she thought she would give the little thing a proper wash. Partly this was because of all that sweat and runny poo, but partly she was curious to see how it would react. In the kitchen she filled her big earthenware mixing bowl with warm water and then carried it slowly up to her room. She placed it on her chest of drawers then laid out a clean towel next to it. "Sprout," she said (it was a nickname she had given it) "let's give you a bath." Lately, when she spoke, it would look at her with its inexpressive face, ready to see what would happen next. She picked Sprout up gently from the bed, supporting its bottom and torso; it could hold its head erect now. She laid it on the towel next to the bowl so it could get used to where it was. It gazed around the room from its new vantage point, mute and calm as usual. She picked it up again, holding it upright over the bowl so that its feet barely touched the water. It moved them as soon as they felt the water and made little splashes. Was it having fun? The face gave no sign. She held it there, uncertain. She wondered about the temperature. She held Sprout with one hand and wiggled the other in the water. Surely that couldn't be too hot? If anything, it was a bit on the chilly side. Reassured, she lowered it a little more. It kept moving its legs. Did it have some kind of swimming instinct like they say new-born babies have?

She lowered it again so that its toes were touching the smooth bottom of the old mixing bowl. Now its torso started to wriggle. Its legs were not able to support its weight, so she dropped it down a bit more so that it was sitting upright in the water her hands around it so it would not slip over or under. The arms now were moving too. Not rhythmically like swimming but fast and chaotically like a child mucking about joyfully in the water or desperately trying not to drown. As always, it made no sound. It did not call out in joy or fear or even surprise. She felt completely in the dark about what life was like on the other side of those black eyes. What if it was really suffering? Abruptly, she pulled the little thing out murmuring, "There, there Sprout, it's only water."

She laid it on the towel. It didn't move; it just lay there

on its back. It looked a bit weird, even for a mutant pumpkin-human hybrid, sort of too fat and puffy. She patted it dry with the loose end of the towel. It was hard to dry off. It was sweating profusely; as soon as she dabbed it dry, its skin would start gleaming with moisture. She wondered if it had somehow absorbed water through its skin, like a bendy carrot made plump again by a soaking.

Gradually as she kept patting it, the swollen look reduced until it was back to normal. There was a ghost of a frown on its face, the first expression she had ever been able to identify. It looked feebler than she had seen it for a long time. Baths, on reflection, were best avoided. A quick wipe with a soft cloth would be better. It occurred to her that she had hurt it or harmed it. A surge of guilt made her flush hotly. She had meant no harm. How was she supposed to have known? It wasn't like there were NHS guidelines. All of a sudden, her guilt fired into crossness. How the hell was she supposed to know what to do? She stared angrily at the tiny blank sweaty face. Its eyes were closed. Its chest was rising rapidly with the intake of minute puffs of air, ribs like fish bones supporting the space around some invisible spongy organs. It had curled up on its side, whitish and glistening. It was so alien. She imagined picking up the heavy bowl and crushing it like a slug under her boot, wrapping the mess in the towel without looking and putting the whole lot in the bin. She could be done with it. It wouldn't even cry out and no one would know. The walls and furniture stood soundlessly around, bearing no witness.

The moment passed. How many evils have been left undone by the grace of a moment's pause? Who can count the lives of kittens and babies saved by hesitation? Just a moment separates the murderer from the responsible citizen.

Monica gathered up the moist Sprout and bundled him gently into the makeshift carrier where he settled damply under her fleece as she went out into the garden to clear her thoughts and tend her plants.

As she went from plant to plant, Sprout's perplexed face appeared in her mind's eye. There was something about it. Transformed by that expression it looked not only more human; it looked familiar. Was it her mother's face, irritated by something she had done, that it resembled? Or Kate's, frustrated by the refusal of a treat? She must be imagining it.

The days slipped by. The cold bit deeper in the ground. Ice sparkled expensively on the crinkled edges of tattered leaves. The grass crunched underfoot, as though it was made of thin, fragile glass towers. The garden crystallised into a brittle mineral place. Yet inside the compost heap the steamy exhalations of worms and fungi as they digested the wilted, dismembered plants that Monica had thrown there kept a warm core of life going through the winter. Underneath the old rug that topped off the pile, a limber young slow worm, shiny and smooth, had dug down into its first winter burrow to sleep away starvation in the frostless upper layers of the pile. It dreamt slow dreams of plump spiders and muscular, moist slugs parading before it in a steady snacky procession.

An Invitation

On December the 20th, the day after the end of term, Beth and Jad knocked on Monica's door. They waited, fidgeting, until the door opened a little and then all the way.

"Hello, you two," said Monica, remembering them chilly and fearful from their escapade the previous summer. Today they looked warmly wrapped but nervous, jiggling around on her doorstep. She stepped out, half closing the door behind her to keep the warmth in the house.

"Hello," Jad managed. He remembered the sight of her, bulkily outlined by the streetlights in the dark garden and mysteriously benevolent; why had she helped them like that? The secret shared between them was like a bridge that stretched out from both sides but that neither of them was prepared to cross.

"Hello," whispered Beth, shyly observing Monica from slightly behind Jack's shoulder, wondering whether Monica was really a witchy sort of person or a friendly one after all.

"Mum says would you like to come over for dinner on Christmas Day this year," blurted Jad.

"Oh! Well! That's very kind of her," replied Monica, caught on the hop.

"She says it's at one o'clock and there's no need to bring anything," he added, remembering.

"Really, that's very kind of her. Um, I don't know what to say," replied Monica honestly.

She paused, then said, "What do you think I should do?"

They looked at her, bemused by the question. They looked at each other. Jad shrugged. Beth looked blank.

Monica looked down at their shoes. One of the laces of Jad's trainers was untied and spilled muddily to the ground. Beth's shoes were a shiny black with pink stitching, straps across the top of her white socked feet done up tightly. "Yes," she said, surprising herself, "I'd love to come."

The children, relieved only at the resolution of uncertainty, smiled briefly, turned and started away.

"Wait!" called out Monica. "What time did you say?"

Jad turned. "One o'clock!" he called back. "See you." They scampered back to safe territory on the other side of the garden wall. Monica watched them knock on their own front door which promptly opened to disappear them. Then, half-cross and half-pleased with herself, she went inside and made a cup of tea. As she sat down at the kitchen table to drink it, Sprout gave a little wriggle against her belly. She wondered if he was hungry.

Presents

Later that day as she was making her dinner, she visualised herself at Christmas dinner with the family next door. She'd never been in their house before. She imagined it furnished in a modern style. Lots of cushions on a big sofa. Purple and grey, or coffee-coloured? Big print wallpaper on feature walls. Not too tidy; with those kids around there were bound to be toys and scribblings, biscuits under the sofa, crinkly paintings magnetted to the fridge. For the meal, there'd be turkey and all the trimmings. She imagined crackers, hats, Christmas pudding, a glass of wine with the meal. It would be fine. She'd have her dinner and be suitably grateful. It really was very kind of them. Did they think she was lonely? She wasn't that old, was she? To be a Christmas charity case? They were just being neighbourly. They'd said not to bring anything, hadn't they? Still, it would feel odd to go empty-handed. No, she would take them some little presents. Presents! She hadn't bought Christmas presents since Mum was around and then it was only a gift of slippers or some such and whatever her mum had said she should buy for herself, slippers or some such. She'd enjoyed getting things for Kate, though. Nowadays she just sent her some money in an airmail card. Yes, she would buy them some nice, thoughtful presents to show that she too was able to enter into the spirit of things.

Sprout was to go with her on her shopping trip to town. She'd make sure he was ready to settle and stay settled in the sling for this extended trip. She'd have him out and about, crawling around the bedroom in the morning. This was part of his routine anyway now. He would proceed slowly, feeling his way with his little hands as though he were blind. As he meandered around, he would roll out his proboscis and prod around with that. She would put objects on the floor for him to explore: a shiny button, a fork, a rolling pin. Anything new would engage him for a long time in a multi-sensory exploration of sniffing, tasting and feeling. She watched him closely, finding him utterly fascinating. After he'd had a good go on the floor, she would put him on the chest of drawers by the window so that he could gaze out as he liked to do. He would kneel there, palms flat on the glass, face pressed against it. Then she would give him a big feed and he would be content to rest in the sling while she went about her morning business.

Early the next day, with a fed, exercised and wiped clean Sprout in his sling, she walked into town. Until yesterday, she hadn't paid Christmas much mind. Today, as she made the familiar trek, she noticed the fairy lights draped unlit around the neighbourhood trees and shrubs, the Santas climbing up the side of houses, the Christmas trees standing tinselly and baubled in front room windows. It felt quaint and exotic as though she were visiting another country with strange customs.

At the edge of the town centre, she saw that the shops had joined in with the seasonal makeover; even the normally austere funeral directors sported a wide snake of tinsel around the window and a red and white Seasons Greetings sign in a gothic font. A greengrocers had clearly been overcome with goodwill to all men and had a huge real Christmas tree outside with safety barriers around. Others had gone to town with the snow spray spindrift in the corners of their window. She rather liked it.

Unsure what presents to buy, she went into one and then the next likely-looking shop: the gift shop, the clothes shop, the book shop, the hardware store, the toy shop, the pound shop, the posh chocolate shop. She came out of the latter with a nice box of chocolates that she thought would do for the parents (she realised she wasn't even sure what their names were). For the children, it was harder. She knew them a little, but not enough to get really good presents. She fancied the idea of getting them a proper present, not plastic tat from a toy shop, dolly pink for girls, action red and police blue for boys. She returned to the bookshop but was defeated by not only not knowing what books they liked, but not knowing which books they had already read. While she was in there, and thinking that she ought to get home before Sprout wanted feeding, she hit upon it. She would write them a story and make it into a book for them; that way she could be sure they hadn't read it.

As she walked home in the gusty and grey early afternoon, she started to compose the beginning of the story. By the time she reached home, she had it more or less sorted in her head. That evening when all the things that needed doing in the house and garden had been done, she settled down with her laptop by the fire. She had Sprout in the shoebox by her chair so she could keep an eye on him and feed him if he grew restless. The lid lay next to the box so she could pop it on if Jozef came in early from work. Then she started to write.

> Once upon a time, there was an old woman who lived in a cottage in the woods. The children who lived in the village that was next to the woods said to each other that she must be a witch to live so, but they were wrong. She was just an ugly old woman who liked her own company more than the company of the villagers.
>
> In the clearing around her cottage, she grew vegetables and each year kept a pig in a sty at the back. She was a basket-maker by trade. She could be seen most days cutting smooth young stems

from the willow trees that grew by the stream that bordered the woods. These she would leave in bundles outside her cottage to dry. Her baskets were well-known for being strong and neatly made. She made enough money by selling them at the village market and sometimes beyond to keep herself comfortably.

One autumn day, as she was sitting in the kitchen weaving a basket, a stranger knocked on her door. His clothes were ragged and dusty and there were no shoes on his feet, but his eyes were twinkly and his patchwork cap was set at a jaunty angle.

"Please, mistress, can you spare some food for I am hungry and have travelled far." The old woman looked closely at him and saw nothing to object to, so she said,

"Come in, come in. I have some pumpkin soup and rye bread which you can have if that would do." The man said it would do very well and came in. She set the food in front of him and watched him with satisfaction as he gobbled it all up.

"Thank you, mistress. You have done me a good turn with that fine soup of yours. Is there anything that I can do for you? He looked at her smiling, his eyes looking especially twinkly now.

"Well, the pig does need killing. Is that a kind of work you know how to do?"

The stranger said he had killed many a pig in his time and would be happy to do hers since she had shown him such kindness. She gave him a rope, a bucket and a knife and he set to work. He made a quick and neat job of it.

By now it was late in the day, and she asked if he would like to have some dinner before he went on his way. The stranger agreed readily and ate it with a good appetite and many grunts of satisfaction. The old woman watched him, smiling at his simple pleasure. Then he asked what favour he could do her in return for the fine dinner she had given him. She thought for a moment then said, "There is a tree that has fallen over behind my house. It needs sawing and bringing in the shed to dry. Is that a kind of work you know how to do?" The stranger said he had sawn many a trunk in his time and would be happy to saw this one for her since she had fed him so well. So she gave him a saw and a barrow and he set to work. He made a quick and neat job of that too.

By the time the stranger finished, the sun was going down. He said, "Mistress, I have nowhere to sleep tonight apart from the wood, and the autumn weather chills my bones. Would you let me sleep here in your kitchen by the fire tonight?" He had worked so hard and well that she did not have the heart to refuse him shelter, so she agreed and gave him some straw to sleep on and a warm blanket to cover him.

In the morning, he packed up his few belongings into a raggedy bundle. At the cottage door, he said, "Mistress, I must be on my way, but I owe you a service for your last kindness to me. How can I repay you?"

"Well," she answered, "I find that I have enjoyed the company you have given me. Before I felt quite happy to live alone here in the woods, but now I believe I should do better with someone else here with me. I should like a little company now and then, I think."

The stranger nodded thoughtfully. "I must go,"

he said, "but I believe I may be able to help you all the same. Farewell." He turned away from the cottage and vanished into the mist between the trees.

Puzzled, the old woman went back in and set about her business in her quiet old cottage. She lit the fire and put water to boil and started to make a new willow basket from the stems she had soaked a few days ago.

At noon, she set about making herself some food. She took out a pumpkin from her larder to make another batch of pumpkin soup. She put it on the kitchen table and cut it open. Imagine her surprise when she found inside it a tiny man! He was no more than six inches tall. He sat up in the pumpkin, climbed out and stood up straight on the table. Then he made a neat little bow and said, "My name is Sprout. I am at your service!"

Sprout proved as good as his word. He made himself useful in countless small ways: finding lost buttons on the floor, spearing slugs in the garden with a spear made from an old needle, telling stories of mischievous sprites, brave children and evil princesses. From that day on, the old lady had all the company she could ask for and lived out her days in the cottage in the woods, making baskets and listening to Sprout's endless tales of magic and adventure.

When she had finished the story, she reread it. It had sexual overtones, and maybe the pig-killing was a bit much. However, she reasoned, the children wouldn't be looking at it from a Freudian viewpoint and they might well have seen a lot worse than pig-killing in films and video games. She decided it would do. She liked it, in fact, and the disguised revelation of her enormous secret pleased her hugely. It eased the pressure of not saying anything to anybody ever about Sprout. Tomorrow she would do the illustrations.

The following evening, she made some rough sketches of a grown-up version of her Sprout for the one in the story. She gave him a suit, a bow tie and a velvet cap. She also gave him ears, slightly pointy ones. She left his actual number of fingers because, for one thing, it made him easier to draw. For the old lady, she made her thin and wiry to avoid too close an association of her central character with herself. The stranger was a dapper beggar with long hair and a roguish smile, his face distilled from her fading memories of the father of her child. When she had planned her characters, she drew a handful of scenes from the story to go on the pages opposite the text.

The next night, she formatted the story in a suitably large and traditional font and printed it out on some thickish cream paper that she had left over from the order of service that she had done for her mother's funeral. Her illustrations she cut out and mounted on the same card and then she bound the whole thing together by stitching and glueing. When she had finished, it was well after midnight; her eyes were aching and she was cold from sitting up so late. She looked through it page by page one last time. It was beautiful, and she was satisfied.

Presents sorted. She was ready for Christmas.

Jozef is Off

Christmas time is the busiest period of the year for the catering industry with all those work dos to feed and wash up for. Jozef had been working every day. He was glad of the extra shifts as he was saving up to return to Slovakia. In fact, he'd already got his ticket and was now trying to earn as much money as he could to take with him. He hadn't told Monica yet. He'd barely seen her. She had never been chatty, but recently he was sure she was avoiding him, although he did not understand why. Had he said something? Done something? He puzzled over it. He would have asked her, but she barely looked at him these days. He got the distinct feeling she didn't want him around. He started avoiding her too. Eventually, it got to the point that he felt he must talk to her, at least to let her know that he would be leaving. His flight was booked for Christmas Eve, now the day after the day after tomorrow.

He got up around ten most days as he was working until one in the morning, or even later some days. This morning, the sense that there was some task he had to do had disturbed his sleep and roused him around eight. He must tell her this morning if at all possible. He had a shower to wake himself up and wash off the fine layer of grease that he felt had settled on him during last night's hectic shift. The cook, his lover, had been cool and distant since he'd told him he was going away. This both annoyed and upset him. Stupid bloody people, he thought, demonstrating his improved English, as he shampooed his stubbly head. He was glad to be getting away from them.

He got dressed and went to look for Monica. She wasn't in the garden or in the kitchen. He tapped on her door. No reply. He tapped again and said "Monica? It's Jozef." This time he thought he heard a noise from inside.

"Monica? I must speak to you. Can I come in, please?" Again, some kind of noise. He wasn't sure what to do. Had she collapsed? "Monica?" more loudly, "Are you OK?" It was a little, light sound, irregular, a kind of rustling or scratching on the edge of hearing. He wondered if it was a mouse or a rat and his restaurant instinct made him want to find out. "Monica! I'm coming in," he finally said and opened the door.

At least there was no collapsed lady on the floor. Then the sound came again. He stepped into the room to investigate. He had never been in here before and was uncomfortably aware that he was trespassing. He thought the sound had come from the far side of the bed, out of sight unless he moved right into the room. He went further in, treading slowly, wanting to catch whatever it was unawares. On the ground by the bed was a shoebox. He was pretty sure the sound was coming from inside. Had she got a pet? That just seemed really unlikely. Again, a little scratch. The sound was definitely coming from the box. Had she somehow trapped a mouse or a rat in the shoebox? Just possible, he thought. Not a good place to keep a rat though. A rat could easily get out of there. It would be strong enough to push the lid off or, failing that, to gnaw a way out. He hesitated, not sure whether he should intervene.

As he stood there undecided, he heard the front door open. Feeling guilty for having gone in at all, he stepped back out the room, closed the door softly and then tramped down the stairs. "Monica! I was looking for you. I have to speak with you." He told her of his imminent departure. She expressed surprise that he was going so soon. Even so, he didn't have the feeling she would be sorry to see him leave, though she said exactly the opposite. In truth, she was sorry to see him go in many ways, but her need to keep her little monster a secret

105

meant part of her rejoiced that she would no longer have to be sneaking around her own house.

"By the way," he ended, "have you seen any mice or rats in the house? I thought I heard a kind of scratching that might be one. Don't worry!" for she had turned pale at the mention of it, "There are traps at work, I could bring one back for here." If anything, this made her more agitated, but he understood. He had heard that the British were overly sentimental about animals, even vermin like squirrels and rats. She assured him repeatedly that it would be fine and that she would sort it and that traps would definitely not be needed. He shrugged and considered himself well out of it. He went back to his room and started to pack up his belongings, the ones that he wanted to take with him anyhow.

Christmas Eve

Jozef left early in the morning on Christmas Eve. He had bought himself a new backpack and had no trouble in fitting everything in. At around nine, he was ready to go. He went to find Monica to say goodbye. As usual these days, she wasn't around the house or the garden first thing, so he again tapped on her door. This time she called out straightaway, "Hang on!" A moment later, she opened the door and stood there, filling the frame.

"Monica, I'm going now. I just want to say thank you. For giving me a room. I don't know what would have happened if you hadn't. I was in a bad place then."

She stepped towards him, pulling the door to behind her.

"Oh well. That's OK. I'm glad I could help," she said. Then, "It's been good to have you here, you know. I'll miss you." She smiled. "Good luck in Slovakia. I hope it all goes well."

"Me too! I'd better go. I've got a plane to catch, you know!" He smiled too. Feeling that some warmth between them had been restored, he leant forward and offered a hug. She went along with it. Then she pulled back,

"Go on then. Don't miss your plane. Keep in touch."

They went downstairs together and she saw him to the door. Waving a goodbye, she watched him out the gate and along the road, then went back in and pushed the door shut behind her.

Christmas Day

She was woken on Christmas morning by a text from Kate: "Merry Christmas, Mum! xxx".

She put her hand out to feel Sprout's cool little body in the box next to her. It was a bit like sleeping with an aubergine. "Merry Christmas, Sprout!" she whispered, feeling as if she were in a particularly surreal Disney film.

As Jozef had gone, Monica felt pleasantly freer around the house and decided to give Sprout a treat and to take him down to the kitchen with her. She picked him up and carried him down the stairs. In the kitchen, she set him on the table where she could keep an eye on him while she got some breakfast ready for both of them. He explored the worn wooden surface carefully, feeling, sniffing, tasting then moving on. When he got too close to the edge she picked him up and put him back near the middle.

He still moved by crawling but was speeding up. She wouldn't be able to have him on a tabletop for much longer for fear that he would crawl to and beyond the edge while her back was turned. If he fell, would he be hurt? Would he die? He had some internal structure that resembled a human skeleton, she could feel its solidity, but she wondered if it was fibrous and resilient like wood or brittle like china bones. Whatever, she was determined to do her best to keep him in one piece.

She sieved some of yesterday's soup (rocket, potato and butter bean) for his breakfast and poured a tiny portion into his cup. He sat independently, legs straddled around the cup, tiny hands resting on the rim and lowered his head to suck up the food. He had just a little and then moved away to continue exploring. Was it the rocket, she wondered; was it was too spicy? She would try a blander mix later so that he was full enough to sleep in the sling during Christmas dinner. She imagined herself there, full of a secret, tucking into an ordinary Christmas dinner in an ordinary house, making conversation that she hoped could pass for ordinary. Could she do it? She thought she could probably get away with it and, in an instant of considering not going, decided that she must. She realised then she had been drifting away from the human world as she had immersed herself in the quietly fascinating complexity of her garden. Then Sprout had come along, mutely demanding her attention just by his inexplicable existence. Jozef had slipped out of her life, too quickly and quietly. She was becoming adrift from her species like a helium balloon accidentally released from a small hand and moving slowly upwards into the cold reaches of space.

Christmas Dinner Prelude

The whole 'inviting the lady next door' thing had been Mrs Brown's idea. It came to her while she was listening to a radio program about loneliness at Christmas. There were many people who would be eating Christmas dinner alone, they said, people who had no family to go to. They would buy an individual turkey portion at the supermarket, or, more likely, chicken as it was cheaper, and cook it alone to eat it alone. The television would be their only companion on this day that was meant to be celebrated together. How sad that this was how society was, so heartless and selfish! People phoned in to say how they had challenged this and donated their time or opened their houses to those in need and how rewarding they had found it.

Mrs Brown considered her own Christmas plans and felt she would like to be one of the ones who made a difference. Her thoughts went immediately to the lady next door. What was her name? Had she ever known it? She instantly felt guilty that she did not know it. The lady had been pleasant, though not chatty; they had exchanged the occasional remark on the subject of the weather or a missed rubbish collection. She wasn't exactly old, but she lived alone, didn't she? And she didn't look well off by the state of her clothes. Mrs Brown remembered that there had been an older lady there when they had first moved in, presumably the mother. That woman must have moved in to look after her mother and now there was no one to look after her; how sad! She did not look on her last legs by any means and certainly was fit enough to manage the garden from what could be seen across the top of the privet, but it must be a solitary life and so, she imagined, a lonely one. She would invite her for Christmas dinner; it was the least she could do. It would be good for Beth and Jad to see how important it was to be kind and open-hearted. Little Mikey wouldn't mind. She would suggest it to Col and see what he thought.

Col was sceptical but agreed it would be the right thing to do. So the children were dispatched to ask, the invitation was accepted and that was that.

At one o'clock on the 25th December, the doorbell rang melodiously at the Brown-Jones's residence.

"That'll be her!" called Mrs Brown, "Beth, go and answer the door." Mrs Brown had her hands in oven gloves and was poking the roast potatoes suspiciously; they should be done but the oven was so full of dishes they might not have had all the heat they needed. "Beth! Can you get the door, love?"

"'K, I'm going," Beth replied, putting down the gorgeously popular Barbie doll she had unwrapped this morning. The doll's hair glistened with glamour and sophistication as it fell lavishly over her perfect clothes and body.

Beth trotted to the door and twisted the knob hard to make it open. "Hello," she said, then "Please, come in," she added, proudly remembering the phrase at just the right moment. She stepped back to allow Monica to come past.

"Hello again," said the lady, "Thank you. Merry Christmas!" and in she came.

Mrs Brown emerged from the kitchen, apron over her Christmas frock. "Come in, come in! I'm so glad you could come. Come and sit down."

"It was very nice of you to invite me. I've brought a few things for you." She held out two flat rectangular Christmassy parcels.

"Oh, you shouldn't have! Really there was no need, but thank you. Dinner will be about twenty minutes. Col!

Colin will get you a drink. I've just got to get back in the kitchen."

Steps padded on the stairs, and Mr Jones appeared from the slippers up. "Hello! Merry Christmas!" (What was her name? Had Ronnie told him? Probably. He'd just have to get through without it.) He shook her hand warmly. Her hand was cool and firm and she gave him a nice smile; maybe it will be all right after all, he thought. "Here let me get you a drink. Sherry? Wine? Or I can make some tea if you'd prefer." She chose a sherry, which was a relief as he hadn't fancied his chances in the kitchen with Ronnie in the final throes of Christmas dinner. He motioned her towards the living room at the front. Beth and Jad were both in there, sitting on the floor. Beth had gone back to stroking the hair of the new plastic doll; Jad was staring at the screen of a phone. Little Michael was there too, sitting in front of the television, watching a frantic and colourful cartoon. Colin introduced the children, Beth and Jad glancing up and smiling when their names were mentioned, Michael oblivious.

"Have a seat," suggested Colin. The lady thanked him and chose the end of the sofa. "It's great to meet you properly at last," he continued. "We should have done this before, but you know how life is, there never seems to be enough time!" She nodded agreement, smiling. If he was going to ask her name he'd have to do it soon or it would be too late. But Ronnie would be sure to know it, so he'd just ask her quietly when he had the chance.

"I've brought you and your wife a little something and something for the children." She held out a present to him.

Did we get her anything? Ronnie hadn't mentioned it. "Ah, you shouldn't have! Thank you." He decided to open it there and then as it would fill time. The thin blue paper covered with silver snowflakes tore easily. Inside was a rather nice box of chocolates. He was relieved it wasn't anything weird or too cheap or too expensive. Chocolates always got eaten, mostly by Ronnie. Beth and Jad had gathered round, drawn by the sound of ripping paper.

"Ooh! Can we open them now, Dad?" asked Jad. "I'm starving!"

"No, we cannot! Dinner will be ready soon," said Colin, more strictly than he would have done without an audience.

"I've got a present for you and Beth... and your little brother," the lady offered. "Look!" and she held out another present to the space between the two elder children.

"Yay!" cried Jad, still young enough to be filled with glee at anything covered in wrapping paper. He grabbed at it and started ripping it open. Beth stood by, content to let her stepbrother have the privilege.

Inside was a book, but not like an ordinary book. The card on the cover was not shiny and the picture was just black and white. The title was hand-written in elaborate curly writing that was tricky to decipher. Jad stared at it until with difficulty he made out the words "The Pumpkin Child". Weird. He flicked it open. It was a picture book with big writing on one side of each page and a picture opposite, all in black and white. It was a book for little kids. "Thank you," he managed and passed it to Beth. Beth took it and turned the pages more slowly. "I like the pictures," she said truthfully. Colin went over to have a closer look.

"Oh yes, they're lovely... They're hand-drawn. Did you do them?" he asked the lady.

"Yes, I did. I drew the pictures and I wrote the story. It's not very long. I hope you like it."

"I do like the pictures," said Beth. Jad had come back

113

over for a second look.

"Yeah, they're really good," he nodded, appraisingly. "We'll read it," he announced magnanimously. Beth and he sat down next to each other on the carpet and set to work.

"What a brilliant present! It must have taken ages to make. Have you done that kind of thing before?" He was both grateful for a topic of conversation and genuinely impressed. Wasn't it surprising what people were like once you got to know them? He'd have a proper look at the book later, but the pictures certainly looked pretty professional. It could be that she was a famous illustrator. The book could be worth loads if she was. He looked anxiously across at what the children were doing to it, but it all looked pretty calm as their mouths soundlessly worked the words from text to thought. He'd google her later to see if she was a professional once he knew what she was called.

"Oh, it took just a little while. I enjoyed doing it. I haven't drawn in a long time, but doing that has reminded me of how much I like drawing. What a lovely big tree you have!" She was gazing at its tip bent sideways against the ceiling.

"Oh yes, we like to have a tree. Wouldn't be the same without it. Nice to make the place look Christmassy."

Ronnie appeared in the doorway, taking off her apron. "Dinner's ready!"

Christmas Dinner Itself

Jad and Beth dashed ahead and the adults followed, Colin scooping up Michael who complained briefly about being disturbed. The table wore a plain white cloth and was laid and ready to go, crackers at the side of each plate. A turkey and dishes of steaming veg filled the middle of the table. Ronnie admitted to herself that it looked pretty good and was pleased at the chance to share it and show it off. "Come and sit here," she said to the nameless lady, indicating a chair at the side next to Jad who was already waving his cracker around. They all found chairs, Michael being threaded into a high chair between Beth and his father. Once sat down, they pulled the crackers, finding that the lady was willing to read out and guess the cracker jokes and to wear a tissue crown with good grace. It was all going very well.

Colin carved the bird, feeling a proper pater familias pride in the act. The food was handed round and piled in suitable excess onto the plates. Nothing was particularly burnt or cold, though Ronnie realised she had forgotten to buy cranberry sauce and apologised effusively for the lack of it. The lady smiled, paid compliments about the food and made conversation with Jad and Ronnie next to her. The food was eaten heartily, except that the lady appeared uncertain about the sprouts which she only nibbled at and pushed around her plate. She seemed equally ill at ease with either eating them or leaving them on her plate.

"Don't worry about the sprouts. I know not everybody likes them and I think they are a bit overdone. It's so hard to get the veg just right." The lady said they looked lovely, but somehow she couldn't quite manage them.

Dinner was followed, as such dinners are, by pudding. The Christmas pudding was black and steaming, flaming briefly to the applause of the audience. It was well-matured so its sticky innards were hard to identify, a sweet dark amalgam of fruits, fat and spices, doused in alcohol. The adults had a portion and Col declared it delicious. The children refused it warily and asked for ice cream instead.

All the cooking and the cluster of people were making the room quite warm and the windows were misting with condensation. The visitor started to look uncomfortable and to fidget on her chair. Despite the heat, her face paled. "I wonder if I might go out in the garden for some fresh air?" she asked, standing already. She was leaning forward her hands over her belly, as though she was having some problem with her digestion.

"Oh, yes, of course! Would you like a glass of water? It is warm in here. I'll open a window," said Ronnie, rising too.

"Just some air and I'll be fine," repeated the lady. Colin got up and went to open the back door. She followed right behind him and then slipped through the open door into the frosty garden beyond.

Colin sat back down with his family. There was a little silence in which people thought about the person who had just left the room. She was ok, quite nice really and not particularly strange or smelly, as some had feared. Ronnie was relieved that she had not proved to be a disaster since it was her idea to invite her. Colin was pleased that she liked the Christmas tree and intrigued by the book that she had given the kids. Beth and Jad felt relieved that she hadn't said anything about the ladder business. Michael had been a bit put out by the unfamiliar face and voice, but since nothing bad had happened was consigning her to the background of his existence. Nobody said anything about her. Gradually they relaxed and began talking of family things, of presents they had got, what time *Doctor*

Who was on and who should help with the clearing up. Beth and Jad, quite willingly on this special day, cleared the table while Dad put the dishwasher on and did a bit of washing up by hand. Mum went into the garden to see if the lady was all right and Michael was given a favourite toy to play with as he sat in his highchair.

Ronnie found the lady looking better, walking slowly along the flower bed that edged the lawn, touching the seed heads and the leaves that remained and looking intently at all the plants. "How are you feeling? Won't you come back in the warm?" she asked.

"I'm fine now, thank you. Just some indigestion, I expect. I'll be in in a minute if that's OK." She smiled.

Reassured, Ronnie went back in, and put her feet up in the living room. It had been a long day already and it was only afternoon. In the kitchen, Beth and Jad were beginning to get fractious; they'd been up since forever and the strain was showing. "Go out and get some fresh air you two. It'll be dark soon so you may as well go out while you can. I'll call you when *Doctor Who* is on." The children were released out through the back door.

The Secret Garden

Monica turned as she heard their voices tumbling out. They pushed one another half in fun, half in annoyance, laughing to see the other stumble. She wondered if Kate would have been better off with a sibling. She'd been an only child herself and had never been sure if that was a privilege or a burden. Coming into this warm and chaotic household made her think that both she and Kate had missed out on something. Never mind, there was nothing to be done about that now. She felt drawn to the children, though, and made her way towards them.

"Hello," she started, "Did you like the book?" She was genuinely curious.

"I liked it," said Beth, "but I wish it had been longer. I usually read books that are longer. I read chapter books."

"It was great," said Jad unconvincingly, "but I prefer books that are funny. Could you write a funny one next time?"

"Maybe I could," she mused. "So if I wrote a story that was longer and funnier, that would be better, would it?"

"Yes, but this one was good too," said Jad kindly. "I liked the pictures of that weird little pumpkin boy".

"Me too," said Beth. "I wish he really existed. I'd love to have a pumpkin boy to play with. One that was real and could move and talk like in the story."

"Yeah, we could make him a house and teach him tricks. We'd have to keep him a secret though otherwise everyone would want to have him and they might steal him. We could keep him in the shed and go and take him food every day." Jad's imagination was picking up speed.

"I think he'd be sad all alone in the shed. And he'd get really cold. We'd have to keep him indoors and just tell him to keep quiet and not go off without us when we weren't there. We could leave him some toys to play with. Or books, if he could read."

"We could teach him to read!" laughed Jad. "And teach him to skate! I could build him a tiny skateboard and some mini ramps. It would be awesome!" He made swooping motions through the air with two fingers like miniature legs.

"And I could teach him how to scooter! My Barbie has got a scooter; he could use that."

They were both silent for a moment, imagining the fun they would have. Then Jad said,

"But it's stupid. You don't get little people like that. It's just in stories for little kids. Like fairies and stuff. If they really existed, we'd know all about them, wouldn't we? There'd be documentaries or videos and they'd be in zoos or something." He stuck his hands in his coat pockets making it stick out like a sail.

"I suppose so," said Beth sadly.

This was too much for Monica.

"But what if they did exist, but people kept them secret because they didn't want them to be put in zoos? And maybe they wouldn't be quite like in the story. But a bit like it. Maybe they'd be a bit less perfect. A bit weirder."

"Nah, I don't reckon that could happen," replied Jad slowly. "It would be too hard to keep them secret. Everyone would know eventually. Everyone always finds out." As he was talking, his mind returned to the secret nocturnal trip to the garden in the summer that his parents had never discovered.

There was a pause.

"Shall I show you a secret?" said Monica. Was it the sherry talking? Or the shared meal and good humour? Some notion that Christmas should be a time of surprises and wonder? Or a secret that through some metaphorical law of density and gravity had risen to the surface and was on the point of bursting through?

Without waiting for an answer, she turned her back to the grown-ups in the house and unzipped her fleece a little way down. The children edged round and stretched their necks to peer in. Then she stopped and straightened up.

"If I show you, you'll have to keep this a secret. Not tell anyone. Not your friends. Not your parents. Do you think you could do that?"

"What is it?" said Jad.

"I'll show you if you promise not to tell. If you did tell someone, well, I'm not sure what would happen, but I don't think it would be good." She felt like a child-catcher. She felt like she was making a huge mistake but that she had gone too far to retreat. The event had been put in motion.

"We're not supposed to keep secrets; they said at school we should tell," Beth piped up.

Monica paused.

"They're right," she zipped up her fleece. "Don't worry, I was joking! There isn't really any secret." She smiled briefly. "Come on, let's go back inside; it's getting chilly."

"I bet there is! Show me! I'll keep it secret. Honest. Beth, you go in. I'll be there in a minute." Jad was bobbing up and down, looking at Monica pleadingly.

"I won't go in without you. Come on Jad, let's go," she was beginning to feel mistrustful again of this odd old woman.

Monica looked at them both. Pulling out her grown-up manner, she took control. "Come on you two, let's all go in." She walked to the back door. The children followed a little behind, Beth quiet and Jad tutting and sighing loudly with frustration. Once in the kitchen again, there was an uncomfortable feeling between the three of them that Mr

Jones clocked and wondered at. He hoped the children hadn't been rude to her.

"I'd better be off," said the lady rather abruptly, "Thank you so much for having me over. It's been lovely."

"Oh! That's fine. Been great to have you here. Glad you enjoyed it," said Colin, thinking it quite likely now that the kids had done something they shouldn't have. "Ronnie!" he called, quite unable to say who it was who was leaving.

Ronnie was there in a moment. "I'm off then," repeated the lady, "Thank you so much for inviting me."

"It's been a pleasure. Thank you for coming," smiled Ronnie warmly, quite pleased with how it had all gone in the end.

More goodbyes at the door. Then the lady said, "By the way, I'm Monica. I don't think I introduced myself properly before. Thanks again."

Boxing Day

Boxing Day at the Brown-Jones's dawned with a mixture of relief and disappointment that Christmas was over. No one leapt out of bed in excitement. It was a day of smallish events.

Beth discovered some chocolates she had previously missed which must have fallen from her stocking in the frenzy of Christmas morning. Later in the day, she found Michael with her new Barbie doll, bashing its perfect head against the hard kitchen floor. She gave him a quick pinch in her anger. He began to wail and she instantly felt sorry for him. Luckily, he still couldn't talk well enough to tell on her. She ran out the kitchen up to her room, taking her doll back to safety.

Jad was busy with his new phone. His parents started to wonder if they should have given it to him. After lunch, they insisted that he put it away and do something else. Put out, Jad found Beth and said, "Let's go and spy on that lady next door." Beth wasn't keen, but Jad persuaded her and out they went into the garden.

As soon as they were beyond the back door, they saw her in the garden. She was cutting some of the bushes with some sharp little cutters with curved blades. Standing close to the privet, they could see through the gaps between the twigs without being seen. They whispered about what had happened in the garden with her yesterday. Jad was convinced that there was something she had been going to show them. Beth thought so too but was less keen on finding out what it was. The air was cold and damp and their feet started to go numb as they watched her snip, snip at some bare bush, putting the sticks in a bucket at her feet. They both thought of their night-time misadventure. It was day now, but they both shared a sense of foreboding.

The bush trimming went on. They had only a small store of patience for this kind of thing and they could feel it ebbing away. Beth was getting fidgety and was on the verge of saying they should go in when the lady straightened up and dropped the cutters in the bucket. They watched closely as she unzipped her fleece and revealed a kind of pouch around her belly. Was that the secret? She took off her gardening gloves and put her hands in the pouch. From out of the pouch she took out something whitish. What was it? It looked like a doll but it had no clothes or hair. Did she have dolls? That was pretty weird. Then, as she handled it, it moved. It turned its head as if to look around. Its arms and legs moved too, not just like the swaying of a rag doll but like the wriggling of an animal. She held it to her like a tiny baby with one hand while she fiddled around with the inside of her top. Then she put it back in and zipped her fleece up. She picked up her cutters and went on with her trimming. Snip, snip.

"Did you see that?" Jad exclaimed in a whisper, open-eyed and grinning. "That's it! That's the secret she was going to show us yesterday! She's got some kind of little person, like in the story."

"It wasn't like in the story. It looked funny and ugly. I didn't like it. I'm going in," replied Beth white-faced. Her voice was quick and cross.

"Beth! Don't tell Mum and Dad. They'll want to report it or something. Put it in a cage in a zoo or I don't know," Jad breathed urgently.

"I won't tell," said Beth. "I'm going in. Come on, Jad."

"I'm going to stay here and see if I can get another look at it. You go in, Beth. I'll be in in a bit."

Beth went in and played quietly with her plastic dolls, and Jad stayed behind the hedge, watching Monica. Now that he knew what she was carrying round with her, he fancied that he could tell it was there by the way she walked and knelt carefully as she worked away in her winter garden. He imagined carrying it himself. He was dying to know what it felt like. He'd love to get a closer look at it. He kept staring at her, willing her to get it out again, but, after a while, she went in the house and did not return.

Seven Magpies

Monica was blithely unaware that her secret was out. She considered she had had a lucky escape in not blurting it out after Christmas lunch, all thanks to the sensible promptings of a sensible girl. Nevertheless, there was frustration too as part of her was dying to share this unheard of thing with someone, just not with the whole world.

Christmas lunch had been interesting. She'd enjoyed it, though she felt a little like she was there on false pretences. She wasn't really a charity case yet.

It had been jolly to wear the hat and share the jokes and quite pleasant to sit at a table surrounded by friendly people and have a meal served to her. Should she invite them over to hers? She didn't think that was what was expected, but she would make more of an effort to be neighbourly since they had been so kind. She could easily pop over with some surplus summer veg. They would surely be happy with that; they couldn't be very well off with Mrs Brown having to stay at home and look after Michael who clearly had some kind of developmental issues. He was too big to be sitting in a high chair and had needed help with feeding.

Now, on Boxing Day, she fell again into her routine. Breakfast for two, exercise for Sprout, then out in the garden. Lunch. As it was a mild day, she went out again into the garden afterwards to finish pruning the gooseberries and generally tidy up. Sprout was getting more restless in the pouch these days and she had to take him out to readjust the sling which was getting rucked up as he wriggled. What would she do when he could no longer be safely and secretly carried around by her? She'd think of something. She hoped.

Boxing Day was followed by the Day After Boxing Day, one further step removed from the glamour of Christmas and into the vagueness of Between Christmas and New Year. Just as she was coming in from the garden for lunch, a rare knock was heard at the door. A strange day for a meter reading or a salesman, she thought. It could be a Jehovah's Witness; they didn't do Christmas, did they? Zipping up her fleece, she went to see who was there.

"Hello," said Jad. Beth was half behind him, looking wide-eyed and uncertain.

"Hello, you two. What can I do for you?"

Jad looked around as though someone might be watching him. "We just wondered, didn't we, Beth? if we could come in?" Jad answered in an over-casual voice at odds with his body language.

Monica was nonplussed. What was all this about? Whatever it was, there wasn't really a reason why they couldn't come in (Sprout was tucked up in his pouch). It would be churlish to refuse them after the Christmas invitation. She wondered if it had something to do with what she'd said in the garden. She really should have just kept her mouth shut. Still, she hadn't actually said anything. Nonetheless, she felt herself flushing as she opened the door wide to them and said, "Of course you can, though I'm not sure there's much here that'll interest you."

Hesitantly, they walked in past her and peered around in a way that would be rude in an adult.

"Let's go in the kitchen. I was just going to have some lunch. Would you like a drink? I've only got tea or milk or water, I'm afraid."

"Oh no. We don't want a drink," Jad said firmly as though that was the last thing in the world he wanted. He was looking around the kitchen in an unusually intent way. He was scanning the shelves and the corners of the room looking for something. Beth was looking at the floor, glancing up at Monica or Jad from time to time to check in with their faces. What was going on?

Then Jad turned to her and said, "That secret you were going to show us, could you show us now? No one else will see here. We've talked about it, haven't we Beth. We won't tell anyone. We just want to see." So that was it! She should have known. Monica was about to deny there was a secret, but, before she could, he added, "You see, we know already. We've seen it. In the garden yesterday. You've got some kind of little person under your jumper. Please let us look. Please, we won't tell."

Shit. Shit, shit, shit. Deny? Get rid of them? Show them? They were both looking at her now, fear and excitement jostling in their faces. "I think you should go," she announced in a grown-up and unfriendly manner. Jad's face fell, then crumpled a little as though he was going to cry. Beth opened her eyes even wider. Monica stepped out of the kitchen past them to open the front door. They moved automatically towards it, not looking at her, as though ashamed of themselves or her. Out they went, scurrying away with their heads down, along the path to the pavement and then down the path next door to their home. She shut the door and stood leaning against it, stunned and trembling.

Later that Day

Surprisingly little happened in the immediate aftermath of the revelation. Monica went through the rest of the day waiting for a bang on the door. Who would it be? Col and Ronnie, the newly Christian-named neighbours? A reporter from the local paper? The police? She did not go out in the garden again that day in case the neighbours had a word over the fence querying some strange story that the children had come up with or in case she saw the children themselves. She knew she had cheated them by pulling out the grown-up card and dismissing them with it. It wasn't fair play, but she had been put on the spot and that was what she had done and that was that. To be honest, she was ashamed of herself. She had built a wall between her and them; the wall had done its job, but left her, like the Selfish Giant, cross and temporarily unable to take pleasure in her garden. She supposed it served her right.

She got Sprout out from the sling and sat him on the kitchen windowsill where he liked to look out at the garden. Or at any rate, he would gaze out at it peacefully for a long time. Monica knew that he could not be observed there from anywhere beyond her garden bounds. She had a good look at him now that his future was once again most uncertain. He was kneeling facing the garden. His hands were on the glass and his face was pressed up against it. He had never given any indication of feeling cold so he remained as naked as the day he was hatched. His skin had stayed creamy white, with just a hint of green to his hands, head and feet. He could both stand and sit in a stable fashion now, though he still crawled to move around. He remained mute. He could hardly be said to be good company. He told her no tales of fairy lands either far away or long ago. Yet he would gaze at her whenever she spoke to him, sometimes cocking his head on one side as though he was interested in what she had to say. However, she had no illusion that the words meant anything to him and was unsure he had much ability to hear at all without external ears. Perhaps there was a gene in his mixed-up DNA that required him to pay attention to faces that looked his way and moved. Sometimes he would mirror an expression or gesture of hers but on a faint, reduced scale. A broad smile would bring a little curve to his mouth and when she clapped, he lifted his miniature hands, but he let them fall down without achieving the reflected clap. She had never seen him repeat those expressions or gestures when alone; they did not appear destined to be part of him. What on earth would he become? What would become of him if the world knew of his impossible existence? She had no idea but felt hollowed out with anxiety at the prospect of it.

Without the garden to occupy her, she felt full of frustrated energy. She busied herself by cleaning the kitchen, cleaning the things that only rarely got cleaned: the greasy outside of the washing up bowl, around the taps on the gas cooker, the toaster clogged up with crumbs. Then she got down on her hands and knees and scrubbed the kitchen floor. All the time she listened out for the noise of intrusion above the sounds from the radio. Yet, as usual, no one knocked, let alone banged on her door. By the end of the afternoon, she almost wished some official had barged their way in and forced her to reveal all. The tension was horrible. It made her want to go round to next door's and dump Sprout in their hands and say it was their turn to look after him. It really was too much. She didn't though. Instead, she made dinner (cheese on toast for her, a tiny leftover of pureed beetroot for Sprout). Then she googled "human-plant hybrid" for the hundredth time and spent unfruitful hours sifting through the fantasies, practical jokes and science for any hint that Sprout and she were not all alone in the world.

By her ten o'clock bed time, nothing had changed. Sprout was there in a playpen made from a cardboard box in which she had placed various items she thought he might enjoy exploring (a raw beetroot, some scrunched up foil, a cotton reel and a toilet roll inner tube). As she hadn't been called to account by some nebulous state authority (Special Branch?), she gave up on the day and went to bed. Lying there, with Sprout passively by her side, she turned on the radio to listen to Book at Bedtime. This week it was *Day of the Triffids* by John Wyndham.

Disclosure

In the house next door there was controversy. Jad and Beth were turning over the options for what to do next, now that they knew that the house next door contained such a weird and amazing creature as a tiny human person. It had taken all Jad's enticements to get Beth to go with him next door to try to get a proper look at it. He had had to promise to play dolls with her for a whole day, though Jad had not actually said which day and was hoping he might be able to get out of it. He was kicking himself for having said to the woman about having seen it in the garden. If he hadn't, they might have been able to catch a glimpse of it somehow. As it was, it seemed impossible that she would ever willingly let them see it now. Even Jad couldn't face knocking on her door again after the way she had told them to go. He felt hot blood rise to his face whenever he thought of it.

Jad couldn't let it lie though, which was exactly what Beth wanted him to do. Beth was closer imaginatively to the world of fairies so it wasn't so astonishing to her that such a thing could exist. Jad, on the other hand, had just put all childish things behind him, Father Christmas, the Tooth Fairy, the Bogeyman, Baby Jesus. This seemingly magical creature ripped open his imagination again. If that existed, what else was out there in the world for him to discover? He wasn't completely sure of what he'd seen, though. He just needed to get a really good look at it. Was it some kind of weird doll or electronic toy that she had because she was a crazy lonely person? That was much more likely, but it had definitely looked alive.

Jad kept up his efforts to persuade Beth (as usual) to help him in a covert surveillance operation. They should stake out the garden and just wait for another look. When they saw it, Jad would take a picture with his new phone as proof. Beth insisted she'd done enough peering through that hedge and that it was cold and boring. Exasperated, Jad said he would do it by himself then and she could stay inside playing with her stupid dolls. Beth claimed they weren't stupid and that he'd get into trouble if he kept on spying on people. That woman next door would do something to him and it would be his own fault. Jad thought she had made a fair point but kept that to himself.

"Well, I'm going anyway," said Jad and thumped down the stairs to get his wellies and coat on. Beth humpfed and went to the corner of the room where she kept her beautiful dolls. She knelt down there and, using a miniature purple brush, smoothed their long shiny hair. She sang a wordless, high-pitched song as she did so, soothing herself.

Jad spent ten minutes or so crouched down behind the privet staring at the adjacent empty garden. Then he decided that crouching, which was pretty uncomfortable, was more than likely unnecessary, so he stood up, his head just below the top of the hedge. He stayed like this for fifteen minutes or so. It was hard work, spying seriously. It was cold and boring, just like Beth had said. It was even more boring when it was just him doing it. The light slipped away with the afternoon. He considered getting his phone out and playing a game on that, but he wouldn't be able to look at the screen and the garden too. There was no sign of the lady next door. A little brown bird landed on a bush in her garden. It hopped from branch to branch then flew off. He decided to call it a day. The lady might not bring the creature into the garden next time she went out there. Maybe she would hide it away in her house, in a cellar or cupboard. That would be sad, thought Jad, who had an instinctive dislike of creatures in cages. Should he rescue it? But to go into that house uninvited was a dreadful idea. She had seemed nice at first, but adults weren't to be trusted. He wondered if Beth was right to be suspicious of her. How had she got hold of that thing anyway? Had she done spells or experiments on children? He shuddered and went back in the warm to think of a better strategy.

Ronnie was sat at the kitchen table peeling potatoes for dinner. Jad offered to help her with the veg and got himself a board and knife. Ronnie gave him a handful of carrots to cut.

"Ronnie," said Jad as he was midway through his second carrot, "how small is the smallest person?"

"Ooh, I don't know. About 22 inches, I think. About this high." She levelled her hand at the height of the kitchen table. "Why don't you look it up? You got that Guinness Book of Records for Christmas."

"Mmm... OK, but when they're babies are they really tiny, like this high. He put his hand six inches above the table.

"No, no, I don't think so. Maybe they're a bit smaller than average, but I think it's just that they don't grow much."

A few minutes later, Jad asked another question, "Can old women have babies?"

"Not when they're very old. Their bodies don't have any eggs left. Why?"

"Dunno. Just wondering. Like the lady next door, could she have a baby?"

Ronnie blew out her bottom lip and stopped peeling. "Well, probably not, I think. What's this all about, Jad?"

"Oh, you know. Just wondering." He bent his head down over his board and chopped the carrots more rapidly.

"And what were you doing by the hedge earlier? I do

133

believe you're up to something, Jad Jones. Please don't bother the lady next door. I'm sure she doesn't want cheeky monkeys like you two staring at her while she's doing her gardening."

"No, Ronnie. Sure thing." Jad knew he'd asked enough for now. He reckoned the woman next door might have had a tiny baby that was a bit deformed. If it was that small to start off with, it might grow up to beat the world record for being the tiniest person in the world. She hadn't looked pregnant, but it was such a titchy thing that he reasoned her tummy wouldn't have had to stick out much. It occurred to him that she could be ashamed of it being so tiny and funny-looking. Even tiny babies had rights though. What if she wasn't looking after it properly? Again, thoughts of investigation and rescue popped into his head. He risked another enquiry.

"Ronnie, if there's a baby and you think it might not be being looked after right, what should you do?"

Ronnie put down her peeler and the potato she was holding and looked at him. "You should tell a grown-up you trust straight away. Tell me, or your dad, or one of your teachers. Jad, are you worried about a baby?" she asked gently.

"Mmm… Not sure. What if I said I was and then it ended up that really it was OK?" he queried slowly, chopping all the while, not looking up.

"It would be fine. No one would be cross with you. Jad, love, what's bothering you?"

Jad was torn between holding on to his precious secret and letting it tumble out. Ronnie's tenderness was hard to resist.

"The lady next door, she's got a tiny baby. We saw it when she was in the garden yesterday. It was under her jumper. It's really tiny! Only this tall." He stretched his hands an Action Man apart. "It doesn't exactly look like a baby though. It looks like a little child, like in the book. You know the book that she gave us for Christmas. Only it doesn't look quite the same. Its face is more weirder. And it was sort of a bit green, I think."

Ronnie couldn't help laughing in relief. She had been steeling herself to phone social services about some neighbourhood family that was failing to cope with a new baby. As he'd started to ask questions about babies not being cared for, she had been wondering if it was someone she knew and if they'd find out it was her who had reported them. She would do it though. It was the right thing to do.

Jad looked horrified at his step-mother as she snorted with laughter. Seeing his face, his mother pulled herself together. "Jad, I'm sorry. I don't know what you saw, but it can't have been a baby. Don't worry, love, there's nothing to worry about. You did the right thing to tell me. I expect she has a toy baby or some kind of pet. Sometimes people who live by themselves get lonely and get attached to dolls and things. That's why we invited her over for Christmas, love, so she wouldn't be lonely." More seriously now, "Jad, I really don't want you to spy on her. She might feel very self-conscious about it. Say hello to her when you see her though. I'm sure she'd appreciate that."

Jad grunted to show he'd heard but he didn't want to commit himself to saying anything yet. What he saw and what Ronnie was saying were at odds and he had to chew over what to make of it all.

Lengthening Days

Time muddled on. The days were cold, but Monica returned to the garden to work seeing as the sky had not yet fallen on her head. She took Sprout with her in the sling but was careful not to get him out even for a moment in the garden. If he got wriggly, she went inside. Some days were rainy and cold and Monica began to feel restless. Even the astonishing becomes mundane in time. Sprout was fascinating, but not, it transpired, endlessly so. She was missing human contact but caring for Sprout constrained her. She would have been happy to have a lodger again, but that was hardly going to work. In the evenings she started watching films and documentaries more. In the kitchen, the radio was always on.

January dragged and then February appeared. The weather got worse if anything. Even so, day by day the light pushed back the dark by another minute or so. Somehow the bulbs knew and cleaved the sodden soil to show themselves in the cold light of not quite spring. Monica had spared the daffodils from her mother's day as she knew the medicine they wrought in the soul, weary by now of the dark and dreary days of winter. Their flat dull green spears of leaves were enough to lift the spirit as the strange frilled trumpets blaring their smell of yellow were sure to be not far behind.

For Jad, the sight of the creature grew hazy and faint. Had he really seen it? What exactly had he seen? His stepmother's laughter had hurt him as though she thought he had been foolish to even think that he had seen something that was so far-fetched. He didn't tell Beth of the conversation with Ronnie.

Whenever Beth thought of the little thing the woman had under her jumper she la-laed the thought away. She did not again open the book that they had been given. She put it on the bookshelf where the books were tightly packed. It was so thin you couldn't really see it at all there unless you looked for it, which she didn't.

Sprout reacted to the increasing length of the days and the intensity of the sunlight by crawling towards the light. When the sun was out, he was restless unless he was kneeling or standing against the glass in the kitchen window. The palms of his hands and the front of his body lost their creamy hue and became decidedly greenish, like celery. When the sun was not shining on the window, he slept or made unhurried explorations of his surroundings under Monica's careful watch.

News from Down Under

On the first of March, Monica got an email from Kate saying that she and Luke were separating, maybe divorcing. Basically, he had asked her to go because he had found out she was having an affair with this guy she'd met online. She was sleeping on a friend's sofa, but the friend wasn't even a good friend and the atmosphere was pretty tense. It hadn't been an affair really, but it had been a fling and she shouldn't have done it and wished to God she hadn't done it, but she was bored and fed up and frustrated with working in the dental practice every bloody day. All her old mates were having babies. So she was coming home. Was that OK? She was looking for a flight that wasn't too expensive. There was one on the 9th, so she'd be back early on the 10th. She'd get a taxi from the airport; there was no need to come on the train to meet her. She was fine apart from the fact she'd just messed up her whole life. Not to mention poor old Luke's. Maybe they'd patch it up, but he, they both, needed some space. She was going to get a job and start again in good old Blighty. God, she could hardly wait.

Monica replied that of course it was OK to come home. That's what homes were for. It would be lovely to see her. It was a shame about her and Luke. These things happened, God knows, and a break would do them both good. Then they could decide if they wanted to give it another go or actually separate. It seemed like it had been ages since she'd seen her; it had been ages. She could have Granny and Grandad's old room. She'd redecorated it not long ago. There wasn't an actual bed in there at the moment but there was a mattress. If she was going to stay for a while, they could sort out a proper bed. How long did she expect to be staying for?

Kate didn't know. It depended on work. She was pretty skint, especially once she'd paid for the flight. When she got a job she could pay some rent money. Would that be OK?

Of course it would be OK. It would be lovely to have her to stay. She shouldn't worry about rent until she was settled.

Making a list

Closing the lid of the laptop as she finished the last email, Monica felt she was in an impossible situation. She was sitting up in bed. It was cold and she did not have much wood left so she had gone to bed early to keep warm. The room looked cosy with just the bedside light on but it certainly didn't feel it. Pulling the duvet higher around her, she thought about and then rejected all of her options. She took a scrap from the pile of paper she kept on her bedside table for making to-do lists and wrote down the options again.

1. Tell Kate she can't stay here
2. Tell Kate about Sprout
3. Hide Sprout until Kate goes

Kate really needed her now. If she was that low on cash, and knowing Kate she would be, she wouldn't be able to find somewhere to live that would be cheap enough to afford until she had found a job and waited for the first salary cheque. The idea that her child was in trouble reignited her maternal instinct. If at all possible (and it was) Kate must be given refuge.

The idea of telling Kate about Sprout was in some ways the best option, yet it was the one that she least wanted to do. She shuddered at the thought of it. She had been on the verge of showing him in a reckless moment to those two children, but this would be different. Kate was an adult and had an adult's view of the world. She might feel it was her duty to report it and, who knows, perhaps she was right? Even now, Monica sometimes wondered if, in the interests of science, she should let experts know about him and let this wonder be part of the world. Monica certainly couldn't insist that Kate didn't act on her knowledge of Sprout's irrefutable existence. It would be her right to do so and she wouldn't beg her to do otherwise. Aside from the issue of protecting Sprout from the assaults of the world, there was a part of Monica that wanted to keep Sprout to herself for her very own. Apart from killing her mother (and who knows how much of that goes on behind closed doors), she had led an unremarkable life. Having Sprout had given her a sense of importance, even uniqueness, that she cherished at her core. No, she wouldn't tell Kate.

To hide Sprout from a person living in the same house seemed in the long term doomed to failure. She had hidden him from Jozef, but Jozef was just a lodger really and she could avoid him when she had needed to. He would never have gone into her room while she was out, for instance. With his work, he was predictably out of the house for long periods, so she and her little mutant charge had free run of the house. Kate would be hanging around the kitchen, going out and coming back on a whim. Kate might go into any room in the house and if she was asked not to, it would only lead to questions that Monica would not want to answer. Monica was not temperamentally given to deceit. Although she was quite capable of keeping her own counsel, she found lying just about impossible even in the most trivial of circumstances. She tried to lie sometimes and planned to lie, but, at the moment of utterance, the intent fell apart and the truth came out. It was almost a disability.

Having again ruled out all three options, she looked for more. She added these to her list.

4. Kill herself
5. Kill Sprout
6. Move out the house with Sprout while Kate is here

7. Do nothing and hope for the best

Whenever in a tricky situation, she always added a suicide option. She found it grounded her and made her feel she always had a choice even when none of them were particularly good. It did the same here. She decided against suicide as the other options, although difficult, were all interesting and she had not lost interest in the world.

Killing Sprout was in many ways the easy way out. If she did kill him, no one would know but her. It could be easily and fairly painlessly done (squishing with something heavy came to mind again). He would be spared future indignity (although his humanity might not be sufficient for this to be a problem, she mused) and pain. She had already done something similar before (Mum). She wasn't sure she would even miss him. However, this option just seemed plain wrong. Evil, even. She thought she could do it, but she would not.

Having resolved this, she allowed herself a look at him. He was lying next to her, propped up on the pillow. He was gazing at the light and putting his hands up in front of his large dark eyes and then moving them away again slowly. He had been doing this for the last week or so. He was clearly developing, experimenting with the world.

Moving out might work. She had enough money to do it for a little while. Yet if she wasn't in her own home, the likelihood of a chance discovery by a stranger was higher. What's more, Kate was bound to ask her why she was leaving and then she was bound to reveal all, knowing her.

Doing nothing but hoping for the best was often a good strategy in life she had found. Instead of focussing on the bad things that might happen if you did this or that, she could open herself to the flow of the universe and simply let events unravel. Then she would play her part as best she could as the situation that she no longer controlled shifted around her. A kind of improvised dancing to music that you have never heard before.

The second list made her feel better than the first. She still wasn't sure what to do, that much was clear. She would sleep on it and let her unconscious work away at the problem. Putting the laptop and list down at the side of the bed, she turned the light off and buried herself down further under the covers. "Goodnight, Sprout," she whispered to the silence. "See you in the morning."

Putting Down Roots

She dreamt that her washing machine (although she no longer possessed one) was flooding the kitchen and she couldn't stop the water from coming out. The button on the front didn't turn it off and the switches and dials had symbols on that she couldn't understand, though she knew that she ought to be able to. It was as though she had aphasia and signs had become meaningless tangles of lines and dots. Mysteriously, the power socket was nowhere to be found though she knew it must be somewhere and searched and searched. The machine just kept churning and spewing water in rhythmic spurts all over the floor. She put down towels and newspapers but the water was too much for them and kept spreading further and further. She knew her mother would be coming home soon and would be dismayed at the mess.

Hang on, Mum was dead, wasn't she? Hadn't she killed her? No, that couldn't be true; that was part of the dream. The washing machine. Was it broken? How had it stopped? But, she'd gotten rid of it after Mum died. Oh OK. Mum was dead. She had killed her. And she didn't have a washing machine so there was no panic about that. But there was some panic about something, wasn't there? Oh yes. There was Sprout, and Kate was coming home.

Coming to, she found that she had worked out what to do. She would do her best to hide Sprout. If Kate found him, then she would play it by ear, and what would be would be.

It was a fine morning: cool but bright with flimsy clouds flowing across the blue sky. It felt like a proper spring day at last, where vegetable life would be coiling itself up ready to pop up. Lightened a little with the relief of having resolved last night's indecision, Monica felt this would be a good day to start sowing seeds in the greenhouse. She pulled on her clothes and got both of them some breakfast. Then she went out to the greenhouse, Sprout suspended in the warm space below her bosom.

She kept her seeds in a biscuit tin. Sitting on a camping stool in the greenhouse, she flicked through them, discarding those that were too old and putting in a separate pile those suitable for planting at this time of year. Sprout wriggled. Then he wriggled some more. Then he kept wriggling and didn't stop. She opened her fleece and had a look at him. As soon as the zip went down, Sprout wriggled even more, clearly wanting to make his way up and out. Could she let him? The panes of glass were misted up with condensation so it was impossible to see in clearly unless you put your nose right against the glass. Putting the seed tin down, she helped him out and put him on her lap. As soon as she did so, he started crawling off. She picked him up at the edge of her knees and put him back where he had been. He did the same again. What was up with him? Scooping him up, she stood and went over to the door to make sure it was tightly closed. This done, she put him on the ground. As soon as he was down, he was off. It reminded her of Kate at a certain restless stage just before she walked; her crawling was well-practised and she could do it at speed on her hands and feet like a bear. Scurrying, he made his way to the side of the greenhouse lined with containers that faced the garden. He was on the verge of disappearing between two of them when Monica again grabbed him up, fearing that she might otherwise lose him, at least temporarily, in the space behind.

She held him still wriggling a little on her lap. What was this? Normally he was a slow and passive kind of character, easily diverted. She lifted him on top of one of the big compost-filled pots so she could see him. Once there, he crawled towards the glass and, just as he would on the kitchen windowsill, he pressed his hands and face against it and became still. She watched him for a while, but he made no more movements. He had got to where he wanted to go. Looking at him there, bending his body towards the thin spring light, he looked more plant-like than he had hitherto. It was perfectly natural, she realised, for him to feel the urge towards the spring light. Wasn't the plant world around her doing the same thing? Even she felt the yearning for it in her animal heart, a residue of shared DNA from the time before the evolutionary tree branched her kind apart from the vegetable world. So she left him there, glancing at him every few minutes as she pottered around. She sieved compost, mixed in sharp sand, filled seed trays and little plastic pots and laid down seeds in the depth of ground they required to lure them from dormancy and put down roots. Sprout stayed put. As she sowed, she wrote the vegetable variety names on white plastic labels and stuck them in the compost next to each type: Little Gem, Burpees Golden, Purple Beauty and more. To finish off, she watered everything gently from a half-size watering can with a fine rose to let the seeds know the time for action had come.

The sun was warmer now and, separated from the cold air outside, it was a comfortable temperature in the greenhouse. She was reluctant to leave this pleasant microclimate, but her stomach was rumbling, so she wiped her hands on her jeans and went to pick up Sprout from the top of the pot. He hadn't moved at all from his spot. "Up you come," she said, as she put her earthy hands around him and made to lift him. As she did, it seemed as though he was heavier at first and then lighter as she picked him up, as if there was some kind of resistance as he left the soil. She looked at him, puzzled by this. His feet had sunk into the moist compost a little and his ankles were speckled with brown flecks. Noticing this, she also saw that the funny appendage at the back of his heels looked different. It was definitely longer and looked very white compared to his greenish feet. As she watched in astonishment, it rolled itself up into a small neat coil behind his heel. She thought of Mercury with his winged feet. She snorted at the weird elegance of it. He looked at her dreamily through half-lidded eyes and made no response.

Over lunch she mused on this new phase of her little charge. Could it offer a way out of her difficulties? She would put it to the test in the afternoon.

Back in the greenhouse they went. The sun had moved round and was not so strong. She got him out the pouch and set him on the ground. Again he made for the line of plant containers. She picked him up and put him on top of the one he had stood in that morning. He crawled to its edge and found his position and was quiet, spread out across the glass. She found herself things to do in there, glancing across frequently to check he hadn't wandered off. Eventually, the sun moved around so there was no direct light in the greenhouse, just whatever bounced off the trees and bushes and clouds around. She had wondered if he would move to seek out the sun. He did not. He remained motionless, rooted to the spot. The sunlight dimmed further until it was as much night as day. Even then he did not move. Monica was feeling the cold herself. "Time to go, Sprout," she said as she lifted him, again feeling a little resistance as his rooticle (as she spontaneously named it) was pulled free. She saw it again coil up out of the way no longer needed.

Over the next few days, Monica got the room, Jozef's room, her parent's room, ready for Kate. She swept and mopped the floor and ordered a new duvet online. She put clean linen on the bed and put hot water bottles in it each night to air it. She bought a colourful woven rag rug from the Oxfam shop in town to put next to the bed on the otherwise plain, pockmarked wooden floorboards. The chest of drawers and wardrobe were still there so she wiped them down and emptied out the fluff from the corners of the drawers. Seeing it through her daughter's eyes, she thought the room looked a bit bare, but it would do. Kate could always get her own stuff once she was here. It was anonymous, ready to be stamped by someone else's personality. She felt unusually fluttery and excited at the thought of having Kate in the house again. How would she be now? They had lived apart for so long and Kate was sure to have changed in some ways but not in others. She was intrigued to meet her again, this time woman to woman.

At the same time, Monica got Sprout used to his new routine. Early in the morning, she would put him in the greenhouse where he would assume a plant-like trance absorbed by and absorbing the light. She checked on him frequently at first and then gradually less so as her confidence increased that he would stay put. She considered leaving him there overnight but did not. At dusk she would uproot him gently and brush the compost off his tiny toes, speaking to him soothingly as she did. He would look at her vacantly, but he would look at her, raising his head so his eyes focussed on her moving face. It occurred to her that if she did leave him there overnight that when she came in to see him in the morning he would have gone too far into the quiet of the vegetable kingdom and the human part of his nature would atrophy and be lost forever.

Five days before Kate was due to arrive, she walked away from town to the garden centre that stood at its southern periphery. It was a decorative hangar of a building prefaced by a landscaped car park. Sprout was with her. She did not like to leave him alone at the house. The weather was overcast making the bowls of spring bulbs on display outside look premature. Their leaves were up and flowering stalks were emerging. They were like horticultural junk food, always tempting but never rewarding. She was looking for something else. She wanted camouflage.

Picking up a basket, she walked past the overpriced giftware and matching sets of garden tools to the covered outside section at the rear. There weren't many veg plants stocked yet. Most of the space was taken up with pansies and primroses. She was looking for a plant that was leafy and quick-growing. After considering peppers (too slow and uncertain) and cabbages (too wide-leaved and likely to attract slugs – would they have a nibble at Sprout?) she found what she thought would do in the herb section: mint. It would put on height in no time and would grow bushy as well as tall. It would do very well planted around the back and sides of Sprout's pot and would soon provide a screen to hide him should anybody (Kate) venture in there. She bought a multi-pack of twelve.

Arrivals

Despite Kate saying she didn't need to be met, Monica thought she would go to the airport anyway. Now that the time for Kate to arrive was nearly here, she was longing to see her only child. It would be too long a journey for Sprout, though, and she didn't want to risk him wriggling so far from home. What was more, if Kate gave her a hug he would get squished. By now she was reasonably confident that he would stay immobile in the greenhouse for the whole day, so she popped him softly in his pot. The mint surrounded him. It had put on some growth already and was almost as tall as he was. In a week or so it would be taller. She breathed in the clean smell of it as her hands brushed against its leaves.

It was a Saturday and Kate's flight was due in a little after one in the afternoon. She considered for the first time since Christmas at the neighbour's what she should wear. She hadn't been beyond Mayham for many months. She hadn't seen Kate since the wedding. There wasn't much choice given the severe wardrobe pruning she had done after her mother died, but she chose the jeans which were in the best condition and a pale yellow T-shirt to wear under her navy fleece and waterproof jacket. Before setting off she had a last look round Kate's room, as it had already become. It looked fine, but she wanted it to look better, so she hurried down the stairs and out to the garden to snap off the first of the sappy daffodil flower stalks. She popped them in a tall glass with water and then up the stairs again to leave them on the chest of drawers. Now worried about missing her allotted train, she slammed the door behind her and strode off towards the railway station some twenty minutes' walk away.

As she slammed her front door, Jad slammed his back

door. He had been off school with a cold for the last three days and had missed the auditions for the school play, Treasure Island. He'd been hoping for a starring part and all his mates had said that he'd be great as Long John Silver. He had practised hopping and aah-aah-me-heartiesing the whole week until he'd been laid low by a runny nose, sore throat and persistent cough. His parents had perversely, he felt, stopped him from dragging himself to school yesterday when the auditions were to be held in the hall at lunchtime. Today was Saturday and it was all over, not just his chance of stardom, but all symptoms of his cold. He'd been moody and grumpy with Beth and Michael and, in the end, his dad had ordered him out into the garden to burn off some energy.

Jad started kicking around an old football on the muddy lawn. He wasn't allowed to kick it against the house in case he broke a window, so he just booted it around the lawn aimlessly. Dwelling heavily on all the injustices that had been done to him, he transmitted his anger unthinkingly to his kicking foot and gave it a much harder kick than he would otherwise have done. It shot through the thinning understorey of the privet and right into Monica's garden. This wasn't the first time this had happened, but it was the first time since Christmas and all that had happened then. He really didn't want to go next door to get it back, but it was either that or not have a football, even a rubbish one. He considered crawling through the hedge. He scoped it out. The grass was wet and, under the hedge itself, was a bare strip of dirt and dead leaves. He would have to go flat on his belly to get under it. If he went back in the house covered in mud, he'd be in even more trouble. He considered going round the side and just nipping in to get it, but the woman was so often in her garden, that it would be just his luck if she caught him and ordered him off. She'd been pretty scary last time he'd seen her. He decided that there was nothing for it but to knock on her door and ask if he could get the ball. He slunk off round the front, kicking the dirt.

Standing in front of her door, he remembered vividly the last time he had stood there with Beth. He wondered about the little baby creature or whatever it was. It probably was nothing. Ronnie was usually right about stuff. But even so... Pulling himself together, he knocked and waited. He waited a bit more, then knocked again, more loudly this time. She must have heard that, he thought, but there was no voice or sound of footsteps. Half relieved at not having to face her and half frustrated at yet another of his plans being foiled, he practised hopping again, just out of habit. Then remembering that there was no point to hopping anymore, he decided to go down her sideway and just get the ball. She obviously wasn't there and couldn't have a go at him as she'd never know he'd even been there. Determined to salvage something from the day, he stepped off the doorstep and headed round the side.

He saw the ball on the patio, just in front of the tatty greenhouse. He darted along, and grabbed it, gathering it safely to his chest. As he stood up, a pale shape in the greenhouse caught his eye. What was that? It looked like two little hands and a squashed sort of face against the glass. He shook his head; must be some weird kind of plant she was growing in there. As he shook his head, the little head on the other side of the glass slowly shook its head too. Jad just caught a sensation of movement and peered closer. The head had two big black eyes and, as he stared at it, it seemed to stare back. He put his finger to the foggy glass where it was, and a tiny hand moved to meet it on the other side. Jad took a step away, stumbled and ran to his own garden. Safely there, he slid down along the wall of the house and crouched there panting.

Monica at this moment was just getting on the train to Gatwick, pleased to have made it after all. It had been a long time since she had taken a train. She got to a window seat and settled herself in for the hour-long journey, looking out of the window at the fields, allotments and gardens that lined the tracks, meditating on Kate as a young child and teenager and what living with her would be like now. The rhythm of the train was soothing and the ordered progression from station to station reassuringly predictable. People came and went at each station stop, observing the necessary courtesies and distances prescribed by society.

As the train pulled in to the ugly, dark platform at Gatwick, Monica's contemplative mood was broken and she felt a stab of nerves. What would her daughter think of her? She had changed a lot too in the time since Kate had lived at home. To Kate, the house would be Granny's house, not hers. She felt self-conscious about how thoroughly she had erased the traces of her mother from it. Would Kate mind? Would she suspect what Monica had done? And Sprout. What would happen if she did stumble across him after all? She left the train, flustered by this rush of thoughts.

Unused to crowds, she felt dizzied by the waves of people moving around on the platform. So many people. She stood against the wall and waited for the crowd to ebb and disperse like foam on the beach before making her way up the escalators to the concourse and thus into the airport. It was brightly lit and full of bustle and noise. She studied the signs and made her way up and down and along to international arrivals, dodging the wheeled suitcases that trailed obediently behind their owners. Once there, she waited with the other relatives and friends behind the barriers as the tired-looking passengers dribbled through the double security doors for their dazed moment in the limelight. Monica was moved by the greetings of loved ones who found each other: back-patting, hugs, warm handshakes, tears and kisses. How would she be when her turn came?

Then, there came Kate. Beautiful, clever Kate. Her hair was pulled up in a bun. She had the same backpack that she'd had when she had set off travelling after finishing university. Monica had bought it for her. Her face was thin and she looked about her anxiously. Monica's heart leapt at the sight of her and she called out her name. Excusing herself, she made her way through the crowd towards her. Without hesitation she wrapped her strong arms around her daughter and gave her a hug, tears welling up in her eyes. Kate melted into her and said "Mum! I'm so pleased to see you." Then they both wept happily, laughing at the tears in each other's eyes.

Two Women

On the train home, they talked of details, circumstances and journeys, but not of the big things. Kate was full of surprise at how small and quaint things seemed. She had come from the end of summer in Perth and spoke of how she was sick of the heat and the drought and so pleased to see some good old English damp, cloudy weather. Her clothes were not warm enough though, even on the train, and she rummaged through the clothes stuffed in her backpack to find extra shirts and tops to layer up with, laughing at herself for not packing more suitable things.

Her skin had a warm, even glow that spoke of sunnier climes and time spent outside. When she smiled she showed off her perfect dazzlingly white teeth, no doubt benefiting from free servicing at the dental hygienist, though Monica had more sense than to mention this. She couldn't help staring at her; she looked out of place on that train pushing through the grey, damp countryside, like a girl who had walked out of an advert for sun cream at a bus stop. She wondered what Kate thought of her. She was winter pale and surely looked older and dowdier than she had when they had last been together at the wedding. She hoped Kate wasn't ashamed of her. Having Kate there was unsettling. For the first time in ages she saw herself how others must see her and judge her and she felt herself care just a little. Her world was tilting on its axis and she wasn't yet sure how she liked it.

They got a taxi from the station back to the house. While Monica paid, Kate clambered out, heaving her backpack out of the boot.

"It's funny coming back to Granny's house and not the flat, Mum. It looks just the same as I remember it," said Kate as she stood outside contemplating it, head to one side.

"I've changed quite a lot inside," said Monica. "Come on. Let's get you in; you still look cold."

She turned the key in the door and went in, followed by Kate.

"Wow! I see what you mean. It seems kind of bare. It looks nice though. I guess you wanted to make changes after Granny died." She dropped her bag in the hallway and made her way from room to room inspecting and commenting on changes and things she remembered. She looked out the kitchen window to the garden. "You've been busy in the garden, Mum. I hardly recognise it. And you've made a greenhouse. Cool!"

"Come and sit down and I'll put the kettle on. Would you like some food? I made some soup and bread this morning."

"Yes, please. I'm starving!" Her accent was different after all her time in Australia, but otherwise she sounded just like the teenager Monica knew so well.

They ate together. As they ate, they probed each other on the more sensitive topics they hadn't broached in public. Kate recounted key events from her marriage. She described her slow disillusionment with the life she had entered into with enthusiasm not so long ago. Monica listened carefully to what was said and not said. It struck her that even if Kate's father had not abandoned her so casually all those years ago, perhaps she too would have had time and occasion to become disillusioned. Her daughter did not ask her advice about what she should do next, nor did Monica offer it. Kate seemed equally annoyed with herself and with her husband. Monica was happy to be able to offer her a place where she could pause her life and take stock.

Kate asked about Granny and how she had been before she died. She surprised Monica by saying she regretted not having come to the funeral. She had slowly come to feel rootless and isolated in Perth and in time realised she only had a small family and, though they were very far away, they were precious. That had happened a little while after Granny died. These events took a while to be felt, she said. Those family photos that Monica had sent her after the funeral had been the trigger. She appreciated how hard it must have been for Monica to be stuck here with Granny while she was so poorly. It was good of her to have done it, not just put her in a home like a lot of people would have done. Did she mind living here alone now?

Monica told her about Jozef but left out the bit about him having been homeless and penniless when he had come to her. She felt unaccountably embarrassed of her charity in front of her daughter. Naturally, she said nothing of the strange contents of that peculiar pumpkin, but she did say how much she had got into the gardening and that it took up a lot of her time and stopped her from being bored. Kate wondered if she'd thought of getting a job after Granny had died. Monica said truthfully that she had not. Should she have? she wondered. It was what people did, after all.

Kate's eyes were drooping though it was only the middle of the afternoon. She hadn't really been able to sleep during the long flight and it was catching up with her. She said she would have a bath and then crash. She hauled her bag up the stairs to her new room, thanked her mum for everything and went to run a bath. Not long after, Monica heard her shut herself in the bathroom and a little while later heard the water drain out again. Then footsteps along the landing and the sound of the door of her bedroom closing softly. Here she was again, listening out to the sounds of someone else moving around the house.

With Kate safely tucked up in bed, Monica went out to the greenhouse in the dim end of daylight to bring Sprout in. All in all, the day had gone well; her daughter was home again.

Departures

Jad was no longer prepared to disbelieve the evidence of his senses, whatever Ronnie said. He just did not know what to do with the thing that he now knew to be true. It wanted to burst out of him. When his breathing had returned more or less to normal, he went back inside, kicking his muddy trainers off at the back door. He found Beth watching TV with Michael. Both of them were staring at it, lips slightly parted. Jad noticed for the first time that they had a similar look to them. "Beth!" he whispered urgently at her.

"Mmm?" Her eyes did not move from the screen.

"Beth! I've got to talk to you. Come upstairs." She looked at him briefly, used to his emergencies.

"K, when this finishes."

"Beth! Come on!" he urged wide-eyed.

"Shhh. It'll only be a minute." Jad waited, jiggling with frustration. Finally, it was over and she followed him upstairs to the bedroom.

"It's that thing we saw next door. I've seen it again. It's really real. Definitely. I saw it move. It looked at me!"

"Oh, Jad. Not that again. I know it's not real. It's just some kind of weird doll. You didn't go over there on your own, did you?"

"Yes, I did! I just went to get my ball back. But I saw it. Honestly, it's in her greenhouse. She wasn't there; I knocked and no one answered so I just went in the garden."

"Well, I don't believe you saw any little creatures. Fairies don't exist, you know." She said this like she was the older one. She was cross with him for getting her to go with him next door last time and then not playing dolls with her like he had promised. She had just remembered

159

the slight now that he had brought up the topic again, and was determined to get her revenge while she had it in her power to do so.

"Beth! Don't be so... annoying!" he said more loudly than he'd meant to.

"Jad! Are you annoying Beth again?" came Colin's voice from the bedroom next door.

"No, I'm not!" Jad shouted back. "She's annoying me!"

"Well, stop it the both of you," I'm trying to work in here." He'd brought work home this weekend to catch up and was already regretting it.

Jad sighed loudly with exasperation and threw himself on his bed.

Ten minutes or so later, Jad got up from his bed and, without a word, left the room. He went downstairs and put back on his muddy trainers. "I'm just going out in the garden!" he called to his dad. Ronnie was out somewhere with Michael.

Once in the garden, he kicked around the football again. He looked over the hedge casually a few times and then aimed a low, powerful kick in its direction. It hit a branch and rebounded at him. Second time round it got through just fine and landed not far from the greenhouse. It was misted up and impossible to see properly into from this angle. Just as before, he went along his sideway to the pavement and down the path to her front door. All was quiet inside the house and on the street. He knocked and waited. Then he knocked really loudly to be sure that if the lady was in she would definitely hear him. No answer. So far, so good. Heart beating fast, he went down the side of her house to the back garden.

His ball was nicely positioned not far from where he had aimed it. He picked it up to make it look convincing and then turned his head to the greenhouse. There it was! He went up to the glass and looked at it. It looked back at him, he was sure. Then it blinked. He gasped and stepped back. The ball dropped from his hands. He turned to run home but didn't. He had a job to do and he was going to do it. He looked for the door to the greenhouse. It was right next to the house. Even though he knew no one was in, he felt as though he was being watched. If anyone asked him he was going to say that he thought that he'd seen a cat that was stuck in there and had opened the door to let it out. It was the sort of thing he would do so he reckoned people would believe him. The door didn't open when he pressed down on the handle and pulled. Was it locked? No, it moved a bit, making a squeak as wood squeezed wood. He lifted it by the handle and the door swung open easily. Did he dare go inside? Fuelled by the frustration of the missed audition and the pig-headedness of his sister, he did.

Inside the air was warm and damp and smelt of fresh earth. He took another step in, towards the big pot pushed against the glass where the thing was. There were plants in the pot, but among them, the little hands on the window could be easily seen if you knew what you were looking for. Another step closer and he could study the figure from behind. Its skin was smooth and whitish green. It looked just like a young child, slim and long-legged, but with no hair. As he looked closely, he could see that there was nothing where its ears should have been. That was a bit disgusting. Unsure quite how to accomplish the next phase of his plan, he said out loud, "Hello, my name's Jad." It didn't react. He put his head round next to the glass to get a look at its face, but he couldn't see much as it was pressed to the glass. Steeling himself, he put a tentative finger out towards it. It didn't react to either the approach or the touch of the finger. Jad felt the weird coolness of its flesh. It felt like rubber. He was gaining confidence at its passivity. "Hello," he said again, a bit more loudly. "I'm going to pick you up, if that's OK. I'm not going to hurt you. I'm just going to take you to see my sister. She'll be very surprised to see you. Then I'll bring you straight back. OK?" Still no response. He gingerly put his hand out and wrapped it around its middle. Nothing. He lifted it up slowly. As it left the ground, he saw and felt the body move in his hand. He jumped and almost dropped it. It turned its head towards him and gazed at him, expressionless. It was really, really weird and Jad felt his courage draining away. Despite this, his hand stayed curled around it, holding it safely suspended in the air. It could not be doubted. Beth would have to believe him. "I'm just borrowing you," he reassured it, "I'll bring you right back." He put the hand holding the creature under the flap of his open coat and turned to leave the greenhouse. He shut the door quietly, remembering to lift it a little to push it back into its frame.

He was out in the garden again. His football was on the ground. He thought for a second and decided to leave it where it was as that was his cover for later when he would bring the little person back. He was acutely aware of the texture of it in his hand. It didn't feel like a doll. Aside from the coolness, it felt like a little animal, like a guinea pig, with layers of skin, muscle and bone, just no fur. Treading softly, he made his way for the second time that day from dangerous territory of next door to the safety of his own house.

He leant against the wall by his back door to ease off his trainers with his feet, taking care not to jolt his prize. It didn't make a sound and wasn't really wriggling, but it would shift its weight as he moved, providing continuous reassurance to Jad that it was definitely, definitely alive. He didn't call out as he went in but instead trod quietly up the stairs to their bedroom. As he went up, he could hear

Beth up there singing in that annoying way she had when she was playing with her dolls. He stopped on the threshold, listening. Then he heard his own breathing; it was coming in long deep gulps. He waited for it to sound more normal and then went in to see Beth.

She was in the corner by the window where the dolls' house was. Her back was towards him and she didn't turn as he entered the room. She was entirely focussed on the small world she had woven with the slender, perfect dolls and their enviable accessories. Her hand was round the waist of one, making her walk with a jaunty gait over to one of her friends who was going to invite her to a pool party.

"Beth," whispered Jad from the doorway. "Look what I've got." She had not yet ceased to be cross with him and was determined to punish him a while longer, so she pretended she hadn't heard.

Jad walked over to her and knelt at her side. He had been out in the garden; she could smell the fresh air on him and feel his aura of cold. He withdrew his hand from under his coat to show her something. Despite herself, she shifted her head towards him to see what it was. It was the thing. He had got the thing from next door. That horrid-looking fairy thing. It looked more like a toy alien than a fairy with its wide black eyes and lipless mouth. As she stared at it, it opened its mouth and out came a tube thing which it swished around in the air like a snake. She gave a yelp and fell backwards, her hands just saving her from sprawling on the floor. "Sssh, Beth, it's fine, Beth, don't worry. I just wanted to show you. It is real. It is alive, isn't it?" said Jad. Although he could see his sister was taken aback, he was glowing with his own daring and wanted her to appreciate it. "I've just borrowed it. I'm going to put it back in a minute. Look, Beth, it's got no ears." He turned the hand that held it so she could see

163

better.

"I don't care. It's horrible. Take it back." Jad was bemused and disappointed at his sister's reaction.

"Don't you want to play with it, like you said? It's like a doll that's alive. It's awesome. You can touch it if you want. It doesn't mind. It feels OK. A bit cold, but it's not slimy or anything. Come on, Beth, it won't hurt you." He brought it towards her so she could stroke it. She leant further away to keep her distance.

"I won't touch it. I don't want to. Take it back or I'll tell Mum. She's just come back," she gabbled.

"You wouldn't!"

"I would and I will. I'm going to count to five and if you don't take it away, then I'm going to tell her." This was a strategy she had recently picked up from her mother. It made him furious to again be treated like a child by his little sister.

"One, two…"

"I'm going, I'm going!" He stood up and went to the door, putting the unadmired creature back under his coat, frustrated once again. It really was too much!

Ronnie was back. He could hear her talking to Colin in the other bedroom. They were talking about Michael, as usual. He slipped down the stairs while the coast was clear and along the hall to the kitchen. Michael was sitting on the floor, rocking backwards and forwards as he often did. Impulsively, Jad knelt down in front of him.

"Mikey? Hello, Mikey. Mikey," Jad said in the soft, high voice he used when speaking to his half-brother. Michael stopped rocking and glanced to the side of Jad's face; he seemed to be paying attention. "Look, Mikey. Look what I've got," and Jad brought the strange tiny person thing out from under his coat. Michael looked and Jad, encouraged, brought it closer to him so he could see it better. Mikey wouldn't tell on him. He couldn't really talk at all, so Jad had no worries on that score. "Look, Mikey, it's moving." It had started wriggling its legs as though it wanted to get down and walk. Jad loosened his grip a little so that it could move more easily.

Without warning, Michael's hand shot out and he grabbed the wriggling legs and pulled. It came easily out of Jad's relaxed grasp. Michael lifted it straight up above him and then brought it down in a smooth movement to impact with a crack on the floor, like an egg being hit hard with a big spoon. Then he raised his arm to repeat the movement. Jad grabbed his arm as it was on its way up and roughly pulled the creature from his grip. He could tell straight away it felt wrong. Too floppy. Its head was broken and wet stuff was coming out from the bashed side of it. Its eyes were open, but they didn't move. Tears rising to his eyes, Jad stuffed it under his coat and ran to the back door. Michael wailed, high and urgent. Jad squished his trainers on, standing on the heels until he had rammed his feet in.

Once outside, he leant against the back wall of their house and took the thing out to inspect it. He wiped his wet eyes and nose with his coat sleeve. Could he mend it with plasters? As he held it out to look closely, it was clear that as much as it had been alive before, it was now dead. It kept flopping over. The ooze from its head was already starting to become sticky. All of a sudden, he didn't want to hold it anymore. He didn't feel he could just drop it though. He'd have to pick it up again, and that would be worse. He had to get rid of it. He had to take it back. Shielding it under his coat, he crept round to next door.

This time he didn't knock but went straight to the greenhouse, heart in mouth, in case the woman came out to find him. He slipped into the greenhouse, willing himself silent and invisible. Feeling he had done not just a stupid thing but a bad one, he put it back on the pot where he had found it. Naturally, this time it didn't stand up straight against the glass. He tried to stick its feet in the soil a bit to make it stay up, but they wouldn't go in; they were all bendy. He used his finger to make a hole in the soil and then put its feet in, pushing the soil against its calves to support it. It sort of worked. He leant it against the glass. It flopped over to one side, but there was nothing more he could do. He suddenly felt he needed to get away. He turned and fled the scene, barely remembering to shut the door behind him.

A Surprise for Monica

Outside the back door, Monica saw a football on the ground. It must be from the children next door. It gave her a start to think that they might have come over to hers to get it and seen Sprout through the glass. She hadn't considered that possibility and reproached herself for her carelessness. All was well, though; the football's presence was proof enough that it hadn't been retrieved. She picked it up and dropped it over the hedge, wondering how she could work round this new challenge.

She headed into the greenhouse, preoccupied with screens and new hiding places. As soon as she looked across at Sprout's tub, it was clear to her that something was wrong. He was there, but all folded up. She reached out to lift him and he came up without the usual resistance. He was floppy and did not respond to her touch in the tiny ways that he would normally do. There wasn't much light in the greenhouse from the failing sun, but she could see that something had happened to his head. It was flattened on one side. She put her finger to it and felt stickiness. She gasped and cradled him against her. She stood still for a moment in shock. Could she revive him? Could he regenerate? She turned on her heel and headed to the house to see what she could do.

What had happened in her absence? She felt a prick of guilt for not having protected him. But from what? It looked like something had attacked him. Had a bird or a cat got in? No, the door had been shut properly when she came in. Maybe a rat had scurried past and knocked him down? He would have just picked himself up though. She really had no idea how it could have happened. Snails? She shuddered at the thought of them climbing over him and munching him alive as he stood entranced and tranquil in the spring light. Or did he just spontaneously break? That was certainly possible. Although he had appeared perfectly formed in his strange way, it was quite likely he was not and there was some flaw in his genes that made this or some other fatal breakdown inevitable. All the time he was alive, had there been a miniature time bomb ticking him through his allotted parcel of life? She cast her mind back for recent signs of disease or discomfort but could think of none. He'd been fine. All these thoughts swept through her head as she carried him in.

With one hand, she fished out a newspaper from the stack under the sink and spread it out on the kitchen table. She laid him on top of it. There was no answering movement from him as she adjusted his position. The overhead light in the kitchen was a fairly dim one; it took a while to warm up, especially in this cold weather. She had to peer closely to see the detail.

His skin had changed colour somehow, though she was at a loss to say if it was more or less green than before. His eyes were open but they were no longer a lustrous black; they were drying off to a blind dark grey. His head looked a mess. It had caved in on one side as though it had been hit with a blunt object. At the site of the damage, Monica could see a dark greyish mass through the open cracks – his brain, she supposed. He must have had one to be as close to human as he had been. The sticky stuff she had felt was clear and had run out of the wound and dripped around his head and onto his narrow shoulders. She looked carefully at the rest of him for other signs of injury or clues to what had happened. She found no scratches or shiny trails. His rooticles hung limply down, not curled up neatly as they would normally be, even when he was asleep. Apart from that and the dent in his head he was intact.

Even in the meagre light of the kitchen's single energy-saving bulb, it was clear that there would be no recovery from this injury. However he had come to be alive, he was now dead. She felt flat and lost. Not sure what else she ought to be feeling, she let herself be practical. He couldn't stay on the kitchen table. She took a deliberate last look at him as though she were taking a photograph. There he lay impossible and dead on a full page advert for discounted white goods. She folded the newspaper over him and then creased the ends up neatly to make a parcel. She got some string from the kitchen drawer and trussed up the package cum coffin so it wouldn't come apart. It didn't take long. She took it up in her hands; it felt surprisingly heavy now he was dead.

Out she went to the garden again. It was darker now, but she knew her way pretty well even in the night. She stood for a moment to let her eyes adjust so that the grey outlines steadied and took on three dimensions, then she headed down the path to the compost heap. Next to the heap she kept a garden fork for mixing the new debris with the old. Putting Sprout's body down on the path next to her, she lifted off the plastic sheet that kept the rain off. She picked up the fork and used it to make a rough hole in the middle of the heap. Through habit, she sniffed in the rich, sour-sweet smell of the innards of the compost heap and felt the warm air rise up against the skin of her face as it escaped from the centre. She picked up the little newspaper parcel and placed it at the bottom of the hole she had made. There it lay, all the weird, complex wonder of it hidden behind, as it turned out, a substantial three-bedroom family home in a much sought after location with double garage.

The sides of the hole were steep and unstable. Unbidden, a dark clump of partly rotted compost fell on top of the body. This didn't feel right. She stood uncertainly for a moment, then she reached in and retrieved the body. She put it at her feet while she filled in the hole with the fork making the top level once more. Back went the rain cover, tucked in around the sides so it wouldn't blow off.

Taking up the fork, she went further down the path away from the house. There was the old apple tree, barely visible, but perfectly familiar. Under its leafless branches, she pulled away the mulch from a patch of ground a little way from the trunk and began to dig. She proceeded gingerly, using touch to avoid damaging the tree's roots as there was precious little light left. It was a tricky task, but she had set her mind to it so on she went until she had dug down a fork's depth. She reckoned that was six foot relative to the size of the body. The greyish parcel seemed to glow in the diminished light so it was easy to see. She picked it up for a final time and placed it in the grave. There was nothing to say and no one to say it to, so after a decent interval in contemplation, waiting in vain for herself to feel an emotion that she could name, she pushed the soil back over the paper coffin. The fork wasn't much good for this, so she knelt down and finished it off by hand. Even in a hole in the dirt, she reckoned the body would rot down easily. There wasn't much to him really. She looked around for some kind of marker and spotted a large lump of flint by the path. She centred it on the disturbed soil.

She straightened up and brushed her hands together to get rid of the worst of the muck. She turned away from the tree to go back in the house. Next door, the lights were blazing. She wondered again how it could possibly have happened.

Coming To

Kate awoke fuzzy-headed and confused in the whitewashed room. The sun was edging the curtains with grey. At first she had no idea where she was. Then she remembered. She was home. In a way. Being at her mum's house, felt like home even though this wasn't where they had lived together. She reached for her phone and saw that it was 8:23. A good time to wake up. Hopefully, she'd get in the swing of the new time zone without too much jet lag. She had a long drink of water from the glass she'd put by the mattress last night then nipped out naked to have a wee. God, it was cold. Didn't Mum put the heating on? Maybe she couldn't afford to. She'd have to check how Mum was managing. She was looking older and different in some way from what Kate remembered, though really just the same too. She got dressed quickly, layering her thin tops and then putting her one thick jumper on top. Then she pulled on leggings before wriggling her jeans over them. The floor was too cold for bare feet so she put on her sandals and made her way downstairs.

Mum wasn't around so Kate poked about in the cupboards, looking for something to eat. She found bread, jam and peanut butter, tea bags, but no milk. The cupboards looked half empty apart from jam of which there were jars and jars stacked up with no labels on. She made some black tea and toast and put the radio on. It was Radio 4, just like it always used to be. The voices sounded so British it was like they were parodying themselves. It struck Kate that living abroad for so long had robbed home of its naturalness; England now seemed like a subtly exaggerated copy of itself. Sitting herself at the kitchen table, she munched her way ruminatively through three thick slices of wholemeal toast. A plummy voice on the radio was discussing Nietzsche peevishly with a roomful of Nietzsche experts.

Kate turned from her own thoughts to gaze out at the garden. There was Mum! She went to the back door and called out hello. Did she want a cup of tea? Yes, please was the response, so Kate put the kettle on again and made a mug for her mum. She put on an old fleece of her mum's that was hanging over a kitchen chair and took the tea outside. Carrying the steaming mug carefully, she picked her way around the muddier bits down to where her mum was, by the old apple tree at the end of the garden. The whole garden had been turned over to fruit and vegetable growing by the looks of things. Kate remembered playing on the lawn as a little girl, looking at the flowers, picking them sometimes. A little bit of her history lost. But Mum had really made a go of things here. You could see the time she had put in. She felt proud of her for doing it so well, all by herself. For the first time that she could remember, it occurred to her that her mother might well have been lonely without her when she'd left. She'd never really had close friends. She hadn't said anything about feeling lonely, but then she wouldn't, would she?

"Thank you, lovely, that's just what I wanted. What do you think of the garden, then?" Monica asked.

"It looks great, Mum. Show me what all the plants are." Kate was more than happy to play along.

Her mum looked older today than she had yesterday. Perhaps she just hadn't looked at her properly before. Kate followed her around the garden and took care to listen as she listed her achievements and tribulations crop by crop. Some beds were bare so Monica told her what she had grown there last year and what she hoped to grow this one. In others, she pointed out the leeks, spinach and kale which had gone through the winter, but would soon flower and have to be taken out. One tidy bed showed the green shoots of garlic coming through, another, stubby winter peas already twisting around wigwams of twiggy sticks. Kate's admiration grew for what her mum had accomplished. She had made her own world here. Kate reflected that she too had made her own world, but it had not turned out quite as she had anticipated. She was acutely aware that she had been the one who had thrown a spanner in the marital works with her infidelity, but it didn't seem to her that her actions were her fault and were scarcely her responsibility. What had Mum just said about the compost heap? With an effort, she pulled herself back to the here and now.

After they'd been all round the garden, Kate said she was going to walk into Mayham to get some shopping. Was there anything she wanted? There wasn't, so Kate went off to get milk, fruit, bread, something substantial for lunch and some warm clothes from a charity shop. She was going to have to be pretty careful with money until she got a job.

Monica was in a bit of a daze. If Kate had been more familiar with her and less self-absorbed, she would have seen it. It was just as well she hadn't for how could she have explained why she was feeling so disconnected and fragile, sad and angry? She had kept Sprout a secret, as much for her benefit as his, and a secret he would have to remain. Not even Kate would believe her description of him and how she had found him nestling inside a pumpkin. She had no taste for digging him up to show his damaged body off as proof of his existence. On the bright side, she thought bleakly, at least she wouldn't have to worry about Kate coming across him and all the unknowable helter-skelter of events that would ensue. The mystery over his death riled her. It was so unsatisfactory to not have witnessed his end. There wasn't even a series of events that she could imagine happening. Was the football in the garden yesterday a coincidence or somehow connected? She just couldn't make it fit together however much she rearranged the pieces in her head.

When she had woken in the morning, Sprout's absence had, for a second, panicked her. Had he fallen out the bed? Crawled off somewhere? Then she remembered, and the panic melted away and the sadness flicked on. She missed her morning contemplation of the strangeness of the universe and the luxurious privacy that she had to enjoy it. There was nothing special about the contents of her bed today: only she and a little microscopic human detritus lay on the crumpled sheets. Her thoughts ranged beyond her room to the rest of the house. Kate was here. She'd forgotten. How could she have? Lovely Kate (how thin she looked!) was here. She would make sure she had a brilliant stay and help her as much as she wanted to be helped. With this positive thought in mind, she felt her energy recover with a surge and she climbed out of bed and pulled on her clothes. It was a fine morning, cloudy, but the sun would burn through by lunchtime.

Seven Magpies Again

Monica stood up from where she had been kneeling on the grassy path and stretched her back. It was about time to pack up for lunch. Kate called out from the kitchen window, "Mum! I'm back. I got some things for lunch. I'll get it ready for us. It'll be about ten minutes."

"Thanks! That would be lovely." Monica knelt down again with her back to the apple tree. Today, she could stay out in the garden as long as she wanted. She went back to weeding out the tiny mouse-haired chickweed that was springing up amongst the garlic. It looked innocent enough but would be rampant if it got a foothold. She grasped the base of each tiny clump with a pincer grip then wiggled it from side to side to loosen its hold on the damp soil. When she felt it move freely, she lifted it easily out of the ground, with fine, flowing, white roots intact. A brisk shake made the soil fall back on the garlic bed, then she tossed it with practised accuracy into the bucket on the path. As she did this, she pictured her daughter moving around the kitchen looking for things, looking at things, making adjustments, feeling her way into the space. As Kate occupied it and, more importantly, used it, she would come to feel more at home there. How long would she be here? Monica wondered. A week? A month? A year? Longer? She hoped they'd get along OK. It would be different than before. They were two women now.

First thing in the morning, she had had a look at her work of the previous evening under the apple tree. The stone marked the place. She removed it and smoothed and pressed down the earth more firmly. Then she hunted out a few more stones to make the spot more clearly marked. She didn't fancy digging round there and accidentally coming across the decayed remains of her strange silent companion. As she busied herself making things right where his body lay, she saw his quiet, pale face in her mind's eye, gazing at her enigmatically, thinking unknowable thoughts.

Monica was so absorbed in her work and her thoughts that she was startled when Kate called again brightly from the kitchen door to say lunch was ready. "Coming!" she called back and got to her feet, wiping her hands on her jeans. The kitchen table was spread with food from the packets that Kate had bought at the supermarket: tubs of houmous and taramasalata, olives, French bread, salad from a bag (now nicely presented in a white bowl), a little dish of cherry tomatoes, and neat sticks of cucumbers and carrots. It looked beautiful, but somehow too perfect for Monica who had been enjoying a frugal life based on what came from her garden. Tomatoes and cucumbers looked all wrong to her at this time of year. This was a time of root vegetables and cabbage. "It looks lovely, thank you," said Monica, choosing part of the truth.

They sat down and ate together, speaking sometimes. Kate noticed that her mum was a bit distracted; she would gaze out the window then suddenly look down as though she was recalling herself. She couldn't work out if this was just the way her mum was now, or if there was something on her mind. As they came to the end of their shared meal, she asked, "Mum, are you OK? You seem a bit… I don't know, not quite on form."

"Really? No I'm fine. A bit tired, I think," she said quickly. "I'm really pleased to have you here, Kate," she added slowly and deliberately so her daughter would know it was true.

"I know, Mum." Then, "It must have been hard for you when Granny died," she fished.

"Well, yes and no. There was a lot to do afterwards. Paperwork and clearing and things. She was very old.

Her quality of life wasn't much near the end. She had so many health problems, you know. Her heart and her rheumatism. She was in a lot of pain with the rheumatism."

"Poor Granny. I bet she hated being looked after. She always liked to have things done her way. I guess we all do, really."

Monica made a murmur of agreement, and pensively licked a smudge of taramasalata from her finger.

"Kate, I don't expect you to look after me if I get like that, you know. I wouldn't want that to happen. If ever I'm in hospital and they ask if they should resuscitate, please say no. I couldn't bear to be like Granny was near the end."

"OK, Mum. If that's what you want." Then after a pause, "I think I'd want the same."

"Granny was in a bad way before she died. There wasn't much left that was good in her life. I think if I'd been her, I would have topped myself." Where was she going with this?

"Everyone says that, though, don't they Mum? But I don't think, when it comes down to it, people do want to end it all. I mean otherwise they would. There would be lots of old people doing it and there aren't. It's not a thing."

Monica took another of the little tomatoes and chewed it reflectively. It was delicious. But did that make it right?

"I suppose so. I don't know. Maybe they don't find the right day to do it. I guess it's hard to choose a day and say this is it, today and not tomorrow or the day after. Perhaps they just need a little help to do it. A doctor or counsellor they can go to and talk with about it. And a way to do it that's not messy or shameful or painful."

Kate pushed her plate away and gazed around the kitchen.

"I miss her here, at this house," said Kate. "Even though you've changed it so much, I keep thinking of her and Grandad and how the rooms used to be when we came to visit when I was little. I was so far away when she died; I don't think it really hit me properly before. But now it feels like there's a hole where she used to be." Kate's face crumpled and she blew out her breath with a huff to steady herself. Monica went round the table to the chair next to her daughter and put her arms round her while she sobbed. She felt herself coming undone in sympathy and felt tears come to her eyes too.

They sat together like that for a long time. Each enjoyed the old feeling of the touch of the other, so familiar yet translated into a new form by separation and the passing of years. They both thought of Monica's mother and the person she had been. Kate felt she had missed something vital in not being there at the end of her life, like finding the book you were reading had the final chapter torn out. Monica thought of her mother and her foibles, her courage and her weakness at the end of life. She wondered at herself for the temerity she had had to take a hand in events. How had she dared to do it? She must have been mad. Yet, she felt a measure of pride in herself for being so bold. Even now, the fact of having been so audacious and decisive gave her a thrill of life. But here was Kate, wet-faced and shuddering in the aftermath of her tears at the loss. What she had done made no difference to that; her mother would almost certainly have been dead by now even if she hadn't stepped in. Kate would be sad just the same. All she had done was to bring forward the inevitable and spare both of them some anguish. Monica examined her feelings and looked again for guilt in them. Yes, it was there, but it was small and easily dwarfed by the sense that it was both compassionate and rational for her to have taken such an unconventional step as to kill her mother.

Something was not right, though. What was bothering her? She could feel it wriggling its way through the swamp to the surface of her emotional landscape, tail beating frantically to get up to the light and air. Then there it was. She was holding a secret. She was holding two secrets. She had held on to Sprout and locked him away so no one else could play with him. She had killed her mother and not told her daughter the truth. They were both big secrets. Too big to be contained now she was thrust back into the world of other people by this firm, warm contact with her daughter, her beloved, flesh of her flesh, the other that proved that she was not alone. She had to let one secret, at least, go.

"Kate, there's something I have to tell you," she heard herself say. "Something about Granny." So that was to be it.

Kate pulled away a little to look at her mother's face. She sniffed and fished out a tissue from her pocket to blow her nose. "What is it, Mum?"

Monica hesitated, and then, because she had to, went on. "I helped her. I helped her to die."

"What do you mean, Mum? What happened?"

"She was so sad and she hurt so much; I gave her lots of pills at one go. She died that night."

"Oh, Mum! Poor you! Poor Granny! That must have been horrible." Kate's eyes were wide and her face was so close to Monica's that she could feel her warm breath on her skin. "I never would have thought she would have done something like that. I don't blame you for helping her." She spoke slowly, as her thoughts took shape. "Did she go on and on about wanting to do it? That must have been so hard for you."

No, that wasn't right. Could she play along with this? It was half true. Could that be enough? No, this half-truth

179

would be harder to live with than no truth at all, than the silence that had been her shadow since her act.

"No, she didn't. She didn't say it out loud. But I think she was thinking it on that last day. She hinted at it. It was like she had given up. I just couldn't bear to see her like that. There was so much pain and so little pleasure. I put myself in her shoes and did what I would have wanted to be done."

"You mean she didn't ask you to help her with the pills?"

"No." A pause.

"But could she have taken them herself, if she'd wanted to?"

"Yes, I think she could. They were just there on her bedside table."

"She didn't say that she wanted to... to end it all?" Kate was moving further away from her with each answer Monica gave.

"No, she never said it. Not quite like that." Monica was unable to give answers that would have made things easier for her daughter, whose face was looking increasingly incredulous and unfamiliar.

"But, that means you killed her, Mum," said Kate as though Monica hadn't yet put two and two together.

"Yes, I suppose I did. But if you'd been here, you would have seen why I did. I did it for the best, really I did." Monica spoke slowly and carefully, but her voice gradually diminished to a whisper by the time she had finished speaking.

"How could you, Mum? I don't understand." Her tears, so recently stopped, restarted and she put her face in her hands. Monica leant forward to comfort her, but Kate drew away violently. Then, without looking at her mother, she scrambled to her feet and ran upstairs. Monica heard the door of her room pulled shut.

A New World

Monica sat on. There was some relief for her in having outed the truth, but the hurt that she had thereby dealt her daughter felt like a hard stone of pain and discomfort in her own belly. She hadn't considered that this might be a consequence of her actions when she had shaken those fatal pills into the paper cup. At the time she had felt as though the world consisted only of her and her mother locked together in tedium, misery and indignity. She could see now that that was not so, that that was a misapprehension, although a forgivable one in the circumstances. Kate had not been present, she had split off from her mother, from England and made her own life in untouchable Australia. She had not been in the picture.

Should she have just kept her mouth shut and spared her daughter, protected her from the truth? She hadn't needed to know. It was all in the past. It didn't change anything. Yet she felt her world had taken on a new shape in the telling of it. She remained sitting in her chair at the kitchen table, but the room around her was transformed. It became the sordid kitchen of a killer as much as if someone had spray painted "MURDERER" in red paint over the walls.

Monica started to feel the cold, but she didn't do anything about it. She just needed to be still for a bit, she felt, to absorb the reconfiguration of the world. She made an effort to readjust to the new language of gravity on the planet so she could keep walking upright and not fall over. Kate was clearly appalled by what she'd done. What had she hoped to achieve by telling her? Nothing. She had just done what it felt like she had to. The same fearless impulsiveness that had led her to kill her mother, had led her also to confess it. Similarly, she found that, despite the horrible consequences, she couldn't bring herself to regret either her murderous deed or the self-indulgent revelation of it. The past was done and the future would be ground into the present by the whirring unknowable cogs of the universe. There was always and only onward.

She heard a movement from upstairs. Kate. Then it came to her that Kate might feel she had to report her to the police. She wouldn't, would she? The idea of being arrested, questioned, exposed, written about, imprisoned was appalling. She'd rather die. She'd kill herself rather than go through that shame and humiliation. She wouldn't mind being killed for what she had done; it would be an act of Old Testament justice that would deliver a symmetry she could appreciate. It was the journey to punishment that was the object of horror. And poor Kate! How horrible that would be for her to have to turn in her own mother for the murder of her grandmother! It would scar her and define her. Blight her life forever. How could she, anyone, get over a thing like that? For the first time since the murder, Monica was overwhelmed with the feeling that she had done a bad thing. Her crime was not the murder of her mother, but the failure to see that it could destroy the life of her daughter.

Creaks from the floorboards upstairs told her Kate was moving around her room. Would Kate come round? It sounded worse than it was, the killing of a mother. Kate was a sensible girl and a sensitive one. She would be able to put herself in Monica's shoes and realise that what she had done was understandable, maybe even forgivable. It would take a while, but they could talk it through. Monica could explain. What would be the good of going to the police? It would do neither of them and, least of all her old mum, any good. Kate would see that in time, surely.

The bedroom door handle clicked open and then shut. Heavy footsteps trod down the stairs. Monica looked up to the doorway. Kate appeared. Her face was struggling to break free from her control and collapse. She had her coat on, and her backpack was making deep indents on her shoulders. It looked too much for her.

"Mum, I'm going. I can't stay here. Not now. I've just called a friend in London. She's said I can stay at hers. I'm going to get the train."

"OK. I understand. Let me give you some money so I know you're not short." She rose up to get her purse.

"No, Mum. Don't. I'll be OK. I just need to go. I'm going now. Bye."

"Shall I call a taxi? That bag looks heavy."

"No, Mum," said Kate again, more firmly. She turned and walked to the door. Monica followed her.

"I'm sorry, Kate. I didn't mean to upset you. Let me know how you are. Come back whenever you're ready. I'm sorry. I'm sorry."

"Bye, Mum," said Kate as she walked through the door, eyes averted from her mother. Monica stood on the threshold and watched her daughter disappear along the pavement back to the station. Kate did not look back. When she could no longer be seen, Monica closed the door and leant against it, pushing her back into it until it hurt. Then she climbed the stairs to her bedroom. Pushing off her shoes with her feet, she pulled back the duvet and got into bed. Then she pulled the duvet over her head so the light couldn't get in.

Alone at Last

She stayed in bed the rest of that day. She got up to go to the toilet a few times. Once, just as it was getting dark, she wandered down to the kitchen. She got an unwashed mug from the counter and filled it with water and drank it right down. Then she refilled it and took it upstairs with her. The bed was still warm when she got back in it. She took her jeans and fleece off at that point as they were getting uncomfortable. Then she pulled the cover over herself again and stayed there until morning.

In the morning, she considered getting up. There didn't seem much point, so she stayed in bed. Eventually, she felt hungry and hauled herself up to make a visit to the kitchen. Spring sunlight was streaming in through the kitchen window. She didn't feel like cooking. Luckily, there was the food on the table from yesterday's lunch. She sat down and ate the remains of the taramasalata with the remains of the bread, chewing the tough crust patiently. She finished up the tomatoes and the olives mechanically; each time she finished one, she put the next one in until there were none left. The tomatoes didn't actually taste of much in the end, she thought. Hunger satisfied, she got up from the table without clearing away and made her way back upstairs. She opened her laptop to see if Kate had sent her an email. She hadn't. She put the radio on and listened passively to what people were saying about the things that they cared about. She watched the light change the shadows in the room as the sun moved relentlessly across the sky. She dozed off and on. In time, the room grew dark. She slept fitfully.

That night she dreamt that she found the body of Kate as a toddler on the kitchen floor. The body was naked and the side of her head was caved in and flat though there was no blood. She knelt down to look at her and put her fingers on the dent on her head. She became aware of her mother's voice behind her saying that she was naughty and that she shouldn't have broken her. She protested that she hadn't done it, but her mother wouldn't listen. Her mother said that she had to clear up the mess she had made, so she picked up the little body from the floor and took it into the garden. The body was smaller when she picked it up, only the size of a doll, so she could carry it easily. She took it down the garden path to the compost heap and made a hole for it and put it in. As soon as she did, a wave of woodlice came out from the pile and covered the pale skin. She brushed them off, but more kept coming.

She woke up with the dream as clear as a steam train in her head. She was overwhelmed with sadness and lay there sobbing in the early morning light until there was only an empty space where the sadness had been. She drifted back to sleep. When she woke next, the sun had moved on again. The sense of emptiness remained so she got up to eat to try to fill it. Down to the kitchen again. She found a jar of peanut butter that Kate must have bought and ate it with a spoon until she could eat no more. Still feeling like there was a void to fill, looked in the cupboard for more food. There were some oats, so she mixed some up with some cold milk and spooned them into her mouth. When the bowl was finished, she mixed up some more and ate them too. After that she felt she could not eat any more so she took the bowl to the sink and rinsed it out and left it to drain with the spoon balanced on top.

Through the window she could see that it was a beautiful day. The sun was shining and the sky was blue with wispy patches of cloud. There were buds swelling on the bushes and shoots of green breaking through the dark earth. The garden looked at her mutely. She looked back at it blankly. It would have to fend for itself. Turning her back on it, she headed upstairs.

Getting Up

A week after Kate left, Monica woke up from yet another long sleep and thought she should haul herself out of this grey pit that she had sunk into. She couldn't say why she should; it was just an animal sense of meaningless self-preservation that pushed her to make the attempt.

In fact, it was her increasingly strong body smell that triggered her to rouse herself. She had noticed her own odour as it grew in intensity, sniffing with interest at the complex and not actually particularly unpleasant smells floating up from her hairy armpits as she lay dozing hour after hour. The smell was a bit like bruised tomato leaves wilting in the sun. Also, her scalp was getting itchy as fragile plates of dandruff built up. Day after day, a little smudge of grease was pumped along each hair shaft from a hard-working gland just under her scalp. This provided a regular feast for some opportunistic fungi and bacteria that slurped it up and burped and went forth and multiplied. Irritated, her skin remade itself over and over; each new layer pushed off the old in a slow waterfall of dead skin onto her pillow. The sheets were greying too and annoyingly rucked up. She had tolerated it as though it was some God-given punishment. It felt like the sheets had tiny bits of grit on them. She would brush them off with her hand, only for them to reappear a while later from no obvious source.

That morning, her body was too much. She had had enough of this intimacy with her own ecosystem. More than enough. Too much. She got up and ran a bath. While it was running, she pulled off the sour, grey bed linen into a heap on the floor.

She made the water on the hot side of comfortable and

lowered herself in. She shampooed her hair twice. The water became murky with the runoff. She soaped and scrubbed herself from top to bottom. As she rubbed the flannel hard over her arms, fat grey rolls of dead skin held together with grease rolled off. She dunked herself to rinse them and then scrubbed again. She had to soap her armpits three times until they were restored to a neutral odour. She lifted each breast and scrubbed underneath. She used a grey mouse-like pumice stone to deal with the thick skin on her feet. When she had quite finished she stood up and looked at the grey water with grim satisfaction and pulled out the plug. Still standing in the bath, she filled a jug with warm water and poured it over herself to rinse the last traces of soap and dirt away. She shook herself dry as the water drained from around her ankles and stepped onto the bath mat (that too needed a wash, she thought). Then she dried herself thoroughly, appreciating the warmth and rigour of the friction on her pink skin. The bath was covered with the dead matter that had been on her. Kneeling down naked on the grubby mat, she scoured then rinsed the bath.

The bath had done her good. She didn't feel like going back to bed. What else could she do though? The garden, her old refuge, was too close to her, too mixed up in the past that had gone so wrong. She needed space. She opened her mind's eye and saw the grey heave of the sea against a blank horizon. The sea. She would go to the sea.

Now she had made her decision, she felt that she must go there straight away. She dried her hair a bit with a towel and brushed it into a ponytail. Hurrying, she pulled on some clean clothes and grabbed her purse and keys. Kate had still not called her, so she left her phone behind.

Without her thick layer of dead skin to protect her, she felt exposed as soon as she shut the door of the house behind her. She closed her eyes for a few seconds to pretend she was invisible then she walked down the path to the pavement, past the yellow rose bush that was unfurling its tiny red leaves despite her. She walked to the station head down in case someone she knew should be coming along. Her feet moved smoothly along the pavement, one two, one two, like she was on a treadmill and not moving at all. Whenever she glanced up though, she was a bit further along. It was a calm but grey day, the sky blank and flat like a piece of empty paper.

At the station, she bought a ticket to Worthing. She waited for the train, concentrating on keeping her mind a blank. To help her, she tapped her feet up and down or stared at the electronic information board as the present time winked steadily on to meet the time when the train was due. She found herself clicking her tongue with each flick of a second that passed. She looked around. There was no one close enough to notice. She would have to watch herself.

In time, and on time, the train heaved in and slowed to a stop. Monica stood by a door, waiting for the button to flash yellow and then pressed it to make it open. There were plenty of spare seats, so she chose one with an unobstructed window view and planted herself there. She let the train take the strain and absorbed the changing scenery that came into view as mindlessly as she could. Each time her thoughts touched on Kate, or her mother, or Sprout, or herself, she redirected them to processing what came in through her eyes, holding the shapes of things out to herself for inspection of their angles and proportions.

The Sea

After a change of trains at the dismal station at Gatwick Airport, she joined the train that headed west along the coast. She knew the litany of stations on this line: Fishersgate, Southwick, Shoreham-by-Sea, East Worthing, Worthing. The time passed, station by station. At East Worthing she gathered herself together and at Worthing she got off.

The platform looked much as it had when she had last seen it. As always when she found herself here, the shape of the day when she had catapulted herself away from home came to her. On reflection, she had managed fine, until now that is. Kate had gone away from her and she had only herself to blame. Stop. She pulled her focus away from Kate and back to her body. But her body betrayed her; it struck her with sudden clarity as a thing that had been hollowed out; it was an empty vessel just shaped like a human. If someone pricked her with a pin, she would deflate with a slow hiss to a pile of folded skin and clothes on the platform. She shoved the feeling to one side and drew a wall between herself and it. Then she quickened her pace forward through the ticket barriers before it could get her again.

Just like all those years ago, she headed down the roads that would take her to the sea. She kept her eyes fixed on the horizon, or where she knew it was behind the buildings. The streets got crowded and broad, full of shoppers and wanderers, as she approached the sea and the stately and curvaceous pier. Like a matronly arrow, Monica was set to follow her trajectory to the edge of the dry world. She paused to cross the seafront road, even busier now than it used to be when she had lived here. Or perhaps she was just slower and the world around her only appeared to be speeding up.

She wanted to keep walking to the sea and not stop, so she stepped up and onto the pier, skirting the bulge of the concert hall, past a sandwich board announcing a tea dance on Thursday afternoon. She imagined herself briefly at a tea dance wearing a tea dress, though she wasn't sure what one of those looked like, waltzing smoothly with a distinguished-looking stranger. Some other time, some other life. For now, her way was onward. There were few people on the pier on this grey day in term-time. She would rather there had been none, but she did not have the gift of this, so she just looked straight ahead without glancing at them and without exchanging the tight-lipped smiles that passing strangers offer each other when people are sparse. There were paintings decorating the flat art deco midrib of the pier. She would have liked to look at them in a way, but this was not the time.

The little amusement hall blared angrily at her at the halfway point. She had come here with Kate sometimes on rainy afternoons. She had sat her on the shiny motorbikes and in the smooth curves of the cartoon toddler rides without putting money in but making enthusiastic vrum, vrum noises. They had spent hours in there inspecting everything together. She walked past, carefully holding the horizon in her sights.

As she approached the end, the final offering of the pier grew in her view. It was beautiful. A wide round building styled, she had always thought, like a luxury cruise ship from the nineteen thirties and built, like it, at great expense and in blithe ignorance of the coming of war. Now it was stranded out here, becalmed in a different age and struggling to find a purpose. Two elegant staircases wound their way to the upper level, hugging the side of the pavilion like graceful limbs. Monica slowed as she walked towards it, admiring the ingenuity and optimism with which it was built. Modernism was a new age in those days and a modern age was bound, so it was thought, to be better than the past.

The pavilion was wider than it was tall and the pier broadened out to give it space to be walked around and admired. At the far side where the best sea views were to be had, the walls opened out into tall curved windows revealing an empty but luxurious cafe, complete with parlour palms and high-backed chairs. Inside, a gallery supported by white pillars allowed those above to look down on those below. Monica closed her eyes and imagined it full of people from the 1930s, their dark hair set in frozen waves, diaphanous dresses floating as they moved across the floor. Laughter. Smoking. Flirtation. Secrets. She opened her eyes again and felt their shifting ghosts locked behind the glass, like tigers in a zoo. Caught up by the splendour and absurdity of this stranded ocean liner she continued round it.

Before she knew it, she had walked all the way round and was facing landwards. She felt like a comet that had been heading out on an elliptical orbit to the cold dark of unknown space and then found itself slingshotted round by gravity to head one more time towards the sun again.

She stopped walking, resentful of the change in direction that had been manoeuvred out of her. She sagged a little. Then she heard the seagulls' cries around her. They were flying so near to her head that she could hear the air brushing against their wings. They hung in the sky, fearless and strong, using the buffeting wind to keep themselves aloft. They called out noisily, but not to her. She walked over to the railing at the edge and grasped the sea blasted grey wood, arms locked straight, to watch them swoop and dive. She felt a little disappointed with herself. She knew she had been drawn to the sea because of the old consolation it offered of an end to the tension of being alive. Like the girl in *The Red Shoes* she had to keep on dancing whether she wanted to or not, unless she threw herself under a train (or in the sea). She hadn't come to Worthing to kill herself particularly, but it had almost happened. It seemed to her as though there was so little substance to her that she was prey to whims and fancies. Even now, she could do it if she chose, clamber over these railings into the cold, swirling waves below. She was a poor swimmer and would drown without much trouble even if her hardy animal self made the effort to save her from herself. However, she didn't have the will to do it on her own; it was only when hypnotised chicken-like by the distant horizon that it might have come to be.

Poor old Mum, she thought as she gazed at the turbulent surface of the deeps; she had a rough time of it near the end. I don't suppose she minded not waking up. I wouldn't. Still, I should have asked her first, really. She sighed heavily and headed back along the pier towards town.

Just as the sea was giving way to the rattling beach beneath the boards of the pier, she stuck her hand in her jeans pocket. She got hold of her house keys and threw them over the railing into the churning grey water below.

Selling Up

The estate agent at Botts and Basley's Mayham office was delighted to have Monica's house on his books. It was a nice little property, just right for a young family moving up from their starter home. It needed a bit of redecorating and modernising, but that meant the price was set low enough for it to sell pretty quickly. He'd taken the photos of it this morning. The rooms were surprisingly free of clutter which made it look more spacious. The white walls were a bit stark, but that wouldn't put people off as much as wallpaper would have done; they'd just paint over. He didn't take a picture of the back garden as the lack of a lawn might make a buyer think twice. There was a makeshift greenhouse at the rear which was a bit of an eyesore. He had suggested to the owner that she got a man in to dismantle it, but she hadn't yet taken his advice as far as he knew. He'd nip in and check next time he passed that way. She was a middle-aged lady, perfectly pleasant though a bit reserved. Hopefully, once they'd seen the inside they would be keen enough not to mind the work involved in reinstating the garden. The owner wasn't living in it at present (she'd moved to Worthing) so viewings would be straightforward to arrange. No onward chain was always a bonus; it was the bane of his life dealing with all the nightmarish complexity and stressed buyers resulting from a fragile domino line of contract exchanges.

He fiddled around fitting the picture of the front of the house in the hanging frame in the window. He put it in the prime eye-height slot. As he wiggled it in, he mused about how he would remodel the house if it was his. Knocking through the kitchen would be a must. Maybe even a two-storey rear extension if you could get it through planning.

*

Sitting at the breakfast bar in the first-floor studio flat she had rented, Monica opened up her laptop and wrote an email to Kate. It was the first one she had sent to her since they had parted.

Dear Kate,
I hope you are OK.
I just wanted to let you know that I am selling Granny's house. It is on the market at the moment. When I get the money through for it, I'd like you to have it. If you let me know your bank account details I can put it in your account. If I don't hear from you, I will keep it in my account until I do hear from you.
I have moved back to Worthing. My address is 12a Regina Avenue, Worthing.
I would love to see you when you are ready to see me. Just let me know.
All my love,
Mum xxx

It took a long time to write the email. She had started many other ones since Kate had left, but none of them sounded right. This one was OK. In each one she had made an attempt to say she was sorry, but couldn't quite put in that frame the thing that she was sorry for. Murdering Granny? There had been no scandalous hauling off to the police station, so it seemed safe to assume Kate had said nothing, at least to the authorities. Even so, she felt it would be madly stupid to incriminate herself in the black and white of an email. Also, she didn't really feel sorry for that, for the killing. What she regretted was the failure to foresee the possible consequences for Kate. Even that was understandable, though; she was only human.

She pressed Send and shut down her laptop. She had rescued it and a few boxes of other possessions from her mother's house before she had shut it up. She had had to use the spare key under the pot of hyssop on the patio. She glanced up at the kitchen clock. It was time to get ready to go to work.

As she stepped outside, she realised that she had too many clothes on. Although it was only the end of April, the sun was hot and bright. She stopped and took off the thick red cardigan she was wearing and hung it across her bag. She was only wearing a loose cotton shirt underneath but that would be enough while she was walking, and when she got to work it would be warm. It had to be.

She walked along the streets that were already becoming familiar to her. There was new growth on the shrubs and trees in the front gardens that she passed. They were unfurling their soft new leaves, bright green and translucent in the sunshine. The spring bulbs were fading but were being superseded by the late spring flowers which would fade in turn as high summer came. Some lilies of the valley caught her eye growing beside a privet hedge. They looked like they should ring like tiny bells if a breeze came along.

After fifteen minutes brisk walk, she arrived at the detached modern redbrick building where she worked. She rang the buzzer so that Sarah or Nicky in the office could buzz her in. "Hello, it's Monica," she said brightly, for that was how she felt this sunny morning. The door made its answering buzz and she pushed it open. The hallway was wide and full of light from the large windows. It looked halfway between an office hallway and one that you would see in a comfortable middle-class home. There was a bunch of mauve and white tulips standing in a plain glass vase on a wooden coffee table on the right-hand side. She put her head round into the office opposite. "Hello, Nicky. The tulips look lovely."

Community service

Monica made her way to the residents' dining room and through there to the kitchen. Everything looked in order, as it had done each day she had come in since she had started the job. Jenny, who worked the shifts she didn't, always left it immaculate. Monica always returned the favour. It was a kind of pressure, as well as a competition that she didn't want to lose. It was also an act of consideration for your fellow human being.

She washed her hands at the hand-washing sink, taking care to scrub right up to her wrists and down under her nails. The paper towels needed reordering soon; she would let them know in the office on her way out. She tied on a fresh apron from the bottom drawer. As she did this, she scanned the weekly menu on the wall to see what was to be for lunch today. Shepherd's pie with boiled carrots and broccoli: pretty straightforward. She checked in the veg store and the fridge to make sure all the fresh ingredients were there, if not she would have to nip out and get some with petty cash which would make getting everything ready in time for lunch a bit of a rush. All good, so she unrolled the top of a brown paper sack and bent down to lift out handfuls of earthy potatoes. She dropped each double handed load into a stainless steel bowl at her feet. Enough for twenty, but twenty old people who would feel dismayed by a great pile of food on their plates. They liked to finish their dinners and then have room for pudding and maybe a biscuit or two with their tea. By and large, they abhorred waste, especially food waste. She wondered whether her generation, even further from the privations of war and post-war austerity, would be the same.

She tipped the potatoes into the sink and filled it with

water to wash off the worst of the dirt. Her hands moved through the darkening water and rolled the potatoes around a few times; she felt the grittiness build up at the bottom of the sink. Next, she fetched a big colander and set it on the draining board and scooped the potatoes out of the black water to drain. As they did so, she got out the brown chopping board, peeler and a veg knife and half-filled a large pan with cold water. Quiet sounds of conversation drifted in from the rooms around her which she tuned into, picking up bits of information about who had been doing or was going to do what. She set up her station on the counter next to the potatoes. One by one, she transformed the pile of earth-stained potatoes to a mound of neat, creamy chunks that filled the pan. With both hands she lifted it over to the cooker.

While the potatoes were boiling, she prepped the onions. Tears filled her eyes as she tore at their skin with her fingernails and she wept. As she wept, she allowed herself to think of all the sadness in her life. She touched each tender place with her mind to see how much it still hurt. The casual abandonment by Kate's father was reduced to a dull ache of humiliation. The dreadful day when she had killed her mother was like a dry lump of pain in her liver. The lonely death of Sprout was a loss made sharper as she bore it alone. Worst of all was how she had caused Kate heartache and who knows how many sleepless nights when she had come to her for refuge. Monica had done some bad things and some bad things had been done to her. She fished out a tissue from a packet in her bag hanging on the back of the kitchen door and stepped out of the kitchen into the dining room. It was empty apart from John who was reading a paper on the far side by the window. She wiped her eyes and blew her nose hard. John looked up at the noise and she raised her hand and smiled in greeting and admission.

She went back in the kitchen, threw the tissue in the bin and washed her hands again in the little sink. She liked to comply with food safety procedures by the letter; it gave her a satisfying sense of doing the right thing and respecting both herself and the residents.

Recovering herself, she poured some oil in the bottom of the best big pan and turned on the gas. Waiting for it to heat up, she hovered over it with the onions waiting for the smell and viscosity of the oil to tell her when was the right time. A tester piece bubbled straightaway so she pushed the rest in with the blade of a big knife. She mixed them round as they sizzled, a fragrant steam already starting to form. On went the lid and then she turned the gas down to just above the lowest setting. Finely chopped celery next. Then, when the onions and celery were nearly soft, two big packs of fat marbled mince. She inhaled deeply the rich smell as the mince changed from pink to grey in the heat, turning the mixture with a wooden spatula so every bit got its required contact with the hot bottom of the pan. She added a little stock saved from yesterday's vegetables, some frozen sweetcorn and a tin of tomato purée. She seasoned the mix judiciously with salt, pepper, paprika and Worcestershire sauce. Mindful of her responsibilities, she kept the salt to a minimum.

She had known she would need to get a job when she moved back to Worthing. While she was packing up in Mayham, she had applied for any that she judged at all likely to take her on given her meagre qualifications and unusual life experience. She hadn't really expected to get the job in the care home, but they were in a fix as the last cook had left suddenly. The fact that she could start immediately was in her favour. The care home was using agency staff which was both expensive and unsatisfactory. Monica's quietly confident manner and homely looks persuaded them that she would be competent and reliable.

When they learnt that she had cared for her own mother, they felt confident that she would understand the needs of their residents. They phoned her back on the same day as her interview and offered to take her on for a two-week trial period and, all being well, to pay for her to get her Food Safety Certificate (Level 2).

She finished the rest of the cooking methodically, keeping an eye on the time. Lunch was served at one o'clock. One of the care staff, today it was Wendy with her mousy face and tight curly hair, came in just before then to help with the serving. Side by side, they plated up, carefully wiping off gravy spills with blue kitchen paper and nudging the broccoli into neat piles. Wendy's children were growing up and her eldest was causing her heartache by smoking dope in his room and skipping college. Monica listened sympathetically and thought, but did not say, how relatively untroubled Kate's teenage years had been. She had much to be grateful for.

As they arranged the steaming food nicely on the thick white plates, Angela and Magdalena took it round to the tables where the residents, with a growing murmur of conversation, had gradually seated themselves in their habitual places. The magnificent Gloria, as deaf and as jolly as they come, could be heard above the rest, relating a story about when her father had come home so drunk after a small premium bonds win that her mother had refused to let him in the house and he'd slept in the coal bunker, emerging humiliated and blackened in the morning.

Lunchtime puddings were easy. Angela and Magdalena went round the tables with a trolley of yoghurts, sealed plastic cups of jelly, and fresh fruit for the residents to choose from. Red jelly was the most popular option with its flavour of childhood parties.

After serving was finished, Monica set to clearing the

kitchen. By then, the first plates were returning, so, with help from Wendy, she scraped them and rinsed them before putting them in the dishwasher. She would rather have washed them by hand, but food safety required the scalding temperatures that the machine alone could do.

When the kitchen was clear, she had her own lunch. By now, the dining room had almost emptied so she had a table to herself. She had the habit of keeping back a portion of what she had cooked for herself so she could check the quality properly. Not bad today, she thought, though next time she would do a thicker layer of potato as it looked a bit skimpy.

She had a little while before she needed to get on with the prep for dinner so she went to the staff room next to the office. It was empty. Monica made herself a sweet, milky coffee. Then, since the weather had stayed nice, she took it out to the garden.

Eloise, one of the residents she had taken a liking to, was sitting in the sun on a bench. Monica walked over to her, concentrating on keeping her cup level. Seeing her approach, Eloise's brown wrinkly face beamed.

"Hello, dear," she said in her high, slightly tremulous voice. "Come and sit here by me." She reached out both her hands to hold Monica's in greeting. They enclosed Monica's answering hand softly. They felt cool and dry.

"Are you warm enough out here?" asked Monica. "I can nip in and get you a blanket to put round you if you like."

"Oh no, I'm fine. It's lovely here in the sunshine. I'm not a bit cold. I've got my thermals on, see?" She pulled out the edge of a lacy neckline from under her lilac blouse to show Monica. Monica sat down next to her on the bench. They sat in silence a while, then Eloise spoke.

"Look at those tulips," she said quietly, as if they might hear her, "Aren't they tremendous?" Across the lawn was a wide border of shrubs and flowers. At the front of it was a dense planting of tulips, mauve and white. Their pale greyish leaves had peeled away and the long, straight stalks each held a perfect goblet of a flower, opaque and flawlessly coloured.

"Yes, they are," agreed Monica.

More?

This is my first book. It might be the only book I ever write. However, if you have enjoyed reading this and would like me to write another one, please let me know via **www.facebook/WhatVenetiaWrites**.

I also write a regular blog with my writing partner Josie Darling. Here's where it is: **plotpartners.blog**

Printed in Poland
by Amazon Fulfillment
Poland Sp. z o.o., Wrocław